THE ROBOT PULLED THE SQUIRMING, SCREAMING MUTANT UP A FULL FIVE FEET IN THE AIR.

Slowly and carefully, like a man deveining a shrimp, the robot pulled the mutant's spine from his back, clipping off the ribs with auxiliary shears along the way. The mutant struggled and screamed, streaming a rain of blood onto the polished floor. When the robot had the spine bared all the way up to the neck, it used its razor shears to cut off the head entirely.

The robot tossed the grisly remnant of the Royal Chiropractor to the BrainGeneral. Torx caught it by the head. The mouth and the eyes were wide open, frozen in pain and horror.

"Regard well the handiwork of the metal at my command!" squeaked the Overlord. "Catch the rebel Maximillian Turkel, BrainGeneral Torx. Catch him and bring him here to my fortress, dead or alive, by the end of a lunar cycle—or the fate that you hold in your hands will be

MUTANTS AMOK

MARK GRANT

AVON BOOKS ◬ NEW YORK

AVON BOOKS
A division of
The Hearst Corporation
105 Madison Avenue
New York, New York 10016

Copyright © 1991 by David Bischoff
Mutant Hell excerpt copyright © 1991 by David Bischoff
Published by arrangement with the author
Library of Congress Catalog Card Number: 90-93408
ISBN: 0-380-76047-9

First Avon Books Printing: March 1991

AVON TRADEMARK REG. U.S. PAT. OFF. AND IN OTHER COUNTRIES, MARCA REGISTRADA, HECHO EN U.S.A.

Printed in the U.S.A.

RA 10 9 8 7 6 5 4 3 2 1

Dedicated to David Bischoff,
with thanks to
Michael Bradley, Elizabeth Martin and
Robert Mecoy

PROLOGUE

The gun jammed.

"God*dammit!*" said the tall husky man with the bullet in his leg. Fucking antiquated machines! These AK-47s were *always* doing something weird right in the heat of action. Especially at times like this, when the distance between capture or freedom, life or death, could be measured in millimeters.

The two-headed mutant snarled in appreciation of Max Turkel's dilemma. Expecting an easy apprehension now of the terrorist who had plagued this sector for the past month, the creature moved forward, chains clanking, the metallic alloy of its armor groaning around its mammoth muscles like tinfoil around a chunky side of beef.

The guard-thing had backed him into a corner of the hangar, stepping over the smoking, bullet-riddled, and spasming bodies of its two associates, but too dumb—or maybe just too stubborn—to know that the same fate was going to explode through the muzzle of the machine gun.

Fate, however—and old weaponry—had spared it, and now Max Turkel, infamous human freedom fighter, dead gun in hand, had his back against the wall.

The mutant roared down on him, electrosaw in one

hand, seven surgically embedded razorclaws on the seven digits of the other.

Nope, thought Turkel. Not good. Not good at all.

He didn't have time to go for his vibrablade or his plain brown-wrapped Bowie knife, or any of the numerous weapons on his body. He'd be sausage by the time he got some decent metal pointed. So he did the only thing he could.

With all his might, he jammed the AK-47 sights first into one of the mutant's two mouths.

The gun rammed down its throat, ripping out numerous teeth along the way.

Then, dodging the thing's flailing weapons, he bounced back against the corrugated tin and charged the mutant, jumping up and executing a dropkick at the last possible moment.

Which wasn't a good idea for a man with a bullet in the meaty part of his left thigh.

It hurt so bad, the attack scream got real, very fast.

For all the good it did, he might as well have just stayed still—or maybe dropkicked a robotank. The mutie staggered back a few inches—but it was more from getting that machine gun rammed down its throat than from the fancy martial arts move.

Blood and mucus and less savory fluids were pouring from the thick, almost neckless head. The head was choking and gagging, bloodshot eyes wide above his stubby, growth-studded nose.

It reached up with the hand it controlled to pull the offending weapon from its mouth—

"No!" grunted the other head.

—forgetting that the hand held the electrosaw.

Sensing the flesh, the electric teeth whizzed on, slicing through skin and bone like Grandma's knife through a warm apple pie.

2

"Teach you to keep your goddammed mouth shut!" barked Turkel through a sarcastic grin.

Blood spurted and calcium sprayed. All in all it smelled like a bad day at the dentist's office. The spasm the saw produced charged it most of the way through the head before the weapon fell from senseless fingers. The freed half of head fell back, held on to the rest of the head only by a flap of skin and muscle. Gouts of red gushed up from severed blood vessels.

Thus did the mutant's dead head become the prettier of the pair.

Turkel didn't stand around and admire the handiwork. He jumped in to take advantage of the stunned and pained state of the remaining living half of the guard. Quickly, he drew his vibrablade from his belt. Can openers, they were called—and with good reason. Given time enough, they could cut through some of the toughest alloys. Fortunately, the mutie's armor was cheap stuff. Turkel judged where the spot was that would do the most good—to the right of the abdomen area, where the guard-thing's solar plexus equivalent—a kind of rudimentary nerve node—was located.

The vibrating blade slammed into the armor, puncturing it and slicing into mutant flesh a good five or six inches.

The big thing's remaining head gasped and was flung back, sending out its death howl. The seven-fingered hand windmilled around. Turkel nimbly dodged, but again forgot about his bum leg. It gave way on him, sending him back the wrong way.

The claws raked along his left arm, ripping the hell out of his khaki sleeve and taking some skin along with them.

The creature jerked once, twice, and then went down like a sack of mutant potatoes.

No time to examine its damage on his own. Turkel knew he had to get out of this fucking place, and fucking fast too.

The plan had been to blow this airport—the New American Air Force's Kansas base—straight to hell, do not pass Go. However, somewhere along the line things got fouled up. The underground Human Liberation Front had managed to blow up a couple of buildings before that plan had fouled up and an unexpected group of heavy-duty ratpack muties had popped up from some emergency hole, straight out of stasis and armed for bear.

They'd all been killed—Fredricks, Morgan, Sheila, and The Slug—in the first foray. Only Turkel and Mack the Truck had slogged their way out of that wall of fire—only to find their assault vehicle reduced to glowing molten metal.

Good old Truck had taken out the rats with a couple of grenades up their asses from his cobbled-together mating of a rocket launcher and a bazooka from one of the old weapons caches the Front had found. But when they'd ducked into this hangar they hadn't known that it would have a complement of two-headed guard mutants on hand, and although this race of muties were some of the earliest and the dumbest (the extra head had been the sorry attempt of some Third World nation to double the race's IQ), they were well-trained mothers. They'd done a very nasty, very fatal number on Truck.

No time for grief, though.

You had to be alive to grieve, and Turkel knew he needed every iota of his energy to get out of this place with half a spark left in the old noggin.

4

Now he limped over the cooling bodies of the guards toward the small prop planes beyond, which was where he and Truck had been headed. Truck was the pilot, not he. But he'd flown a few dozen hours, knew the basics, because Max Turkel had been sure he knew the basics of just about every aspect of weaponry, martial arts, war, and war's machinery. You had to know that to fight the muties, because they had just about everything else in this world. You had no knowledge, you were doomed from Jump City.

He opened a door, stepped out into the night air, and got the full blast of the sirens. They'd been there all along, those sirens, since the Front had blasted that first air base building, but the hangar had muted the sound somewhat. Now, though, they were shrill and insistent in Turkel's ear. They seemed to yowl, "We're going get your ass, Max Turkel, and nail it to the flagpole."

Turkel scrambled for the clutch of planes on a grassy sward. He felt very attached to his ass, and no way did he want any slimy mutie's hand, let alone nail, anywhere near it. He heard the sounds of machinery in the distance. Tanks? Jeeps? Mutated Volkwagens? Fuck, he thought they'd blown all that stuff up! Thank God they'd destroyed the anti-aircraft arsenal on the base periphery, or he wouldn't have a chance in hell of getting out.

The single-prop planes were a bunch of old Piper Cubs left over from way before the Final War. Muties being muties, though, they'd used just about everything from the Old Civilization they could. The aircraft looked somehow at home bathed in the fiery glow of the burning base, swept by a wave of acrid smoke. It was like they'd been waiting for just such a moment.

5

Turkel dragged his bleeding carcass to the plane that looked in the best shape and had the clearest shot for the runway. His arm was not only bleeding bad now, it was getting numb. The wounds were worse than he thought. He paused by his plane, ripped off his shirt, took a quick moment to apply a tourniquet, and then scrambled into the plane. He had to use his arm before it went dead on him.

He took a second to acquaint himself with the control board, found the prop start button, and pushed. Jeez, this was really an old one. You controlled the ailerons with pedals! Still, it looked well maintained and airworthy, and he didn't have time to try out another one, because the roar of those trucks or jeeps or whatever were getting awfully close.

The start button coughed and the prop did a little dance as the motor kicked over, coughed, wheezed, and died.

Turkel didn't have time to curse. He was boosted into action by the wave of new adrenaline that coursed through him like liquid lightning. He tried the button again. With the exact same results.

This time he had time to curse.

The engine sounds loomed, sounding as though they were just on the other side of the hangar.

The fucking *choke*. Of course!

He groped for it, found it, pulled it out, and then tried the starter again.

This time the engine caught. The gas flowed into the chambers of the cylinders, the spark plugs ignited, and the miracle of internal combustion did its duty: the engine started to chug like a champ. The prop spun and growled its urgency for the sky.

Normally, Turkel would let an engine warm up a bit, but that was a luxury he had no time for. He'd

6

just have to play the choke, praying that the carburetor wouldn't flood. Carefully, biting back his pain, Max Turkel let off the brake and let the propeller drag the Piper out toward the runway. He eased it onto the macadam and straightened it out, lining it up away from the fires behind him for the best shot at freedom he could make.

Just at that moment, the mutie pursuit vehicles emerged from beyond the hangar like creatures squeezed up out of hell.

"Stop!" barked a contorted voice over a megaphone. "In the name of His Highest Supremacy, the Emperor of the Americas, halt and surrender!"

"Fuck you, pal," spat Turkel, and cranked the propeller up to the maximum. The blades snarled big bites out of the cooling spring night air and hauled the light plane into acceleration.

Turkel heard a chatter of machine-gun fire and the angry crank of gears stripping as the mutant-operated vehicle struggled to catch him. He kept his attention focused, however, steady on the control panel, watching the RPM dip into the red, mentally urging the speedometer to the speed at which he could hope for some lift and could yank the stick down and put this baby *aloft*.

An ominous pause to the staccato of the guns.

What? thought Turkel. Their guns jam too, huh?

But no sooner had a little grin appeared on his formerly grimacing face than the voice of the machine guns spoke again. A clatter sounded as they punched a series of holes in the fuselage.

"Jesus Chri—"

Pain creased him like a bent playing card.

A couple of the bullets had caught him in the left side. They were like hot pokers jammed just below his heart and rib cage, and suddenly the world got all red and dizzy and tilting. Turkel caught himself spinning toward unconsciousness and put on his interior brakes. With every ounce of his willpower, he hauled himself out of that dark chasm and brought things back under control.

Get me the fuck outta here, plane! he thought.

Even though the speedometer was shy of proper takeoff level, he pulled down on the stick.

For a breathless moment, it looked like the plane wasn't going up. But then, like an answer to his prayers from the God of Revolutionaries, a spring breeze raced along and pushed the wings up just enough to take the wheels off the ground, relieving it of that friction. Gravity thus defied, the plane angled up, climbing steadily if a little wobbly.

A stray bullet caught the tail, but the rest of the machine gun's spit missed; apparently the mutie at the trigger wasn't a real good shot, and the stream that had caught the plane before had been pure luck.

Turkel took it up to five hundred feet and leveled it off, hoping to stay out of radar range. He put the speed up to the max of ninety miles an hour. If he and his attack force hadn't destroyed the fighter planes on the base, he'd be dead falling meat in very short order; the muties would catch him and make short work of him.

But now, he had a hope.

Chances were they didn't have any pilots with them in the ground vehicles. Muties were specialized. Landcraft drivers couldn't fly, and often as not, mutant pilots couldn't drive a go-cart.

When he felt like he had about ten miles on them, he took the luxury to check his own condition.

The pain had ebbed somewhat, but the blood was

red and plentiful. There was no sign of a first aid kit in the cabin, so Turkel had to make do with what was left of his shirt and his undershirt to plug things up a bit.

When he felt like maybe, just maybe, he wasn't going to bleed to death in the next half hour, he took a look at the compass on the control panel.

He was headed vaguely north.

He sighed, dipped the right wing a bit to take his direction a bit more easterly. If he could make it up to North Dakota, he might just have a shot at continued existence.

Then he steadied the bullet-riddled plane and himself, and flew on through the dark and lonely night.

CHAPTER 1

Jack Bender saw the plane at dawn.

Or he thought he saw a plane, anyway. He heard a buzzing first, and he turned from his perch atop the seeding machine just in time to see something sail past the tops of the high trees of Grovenors Forest.

However, the object did not reappear, and the distant buzzing stopped, much in the way a fly's wing sound stops when it has lighted.

Jack turned his attention back to the seeding machine and thought this over a bit. He wasn't a very excitable guy, Jack Bender, and he liked to consider things carefully. Things were slow and steady in farm life, and a guy got used to the luxury of mulling over important things.

The seed machine that Jack Bender controlled was an old thing, patched and colicky, that chunked down soybean sprouts at proper intervals and then covered them over with dirt. Half of Jack's job with this sad hunk of antiquated technology was fixing it when it broke down. Which tended to be about three times a week. Yeah, and it had been almost a week since the last repair work, and there was this pinging sound that would come up once in a while. Jack figured the seeder was just about due.

He reached the end of the row, turned the wheel,

brought the ungainly machine around, and lined her up to lay another line. The air was rich with the smell of damp ground and manure and dew on the grass. You could almost taste the honeysuckle that grew along the sides of the field. The sun had just pushed off from the east edge of Iowa, and the cloudless spring day was filled with light, warming up rapidly. Jack pulled off his sweatshirt and tied it around his neck, trying to concentrate on keeping a straight line with the seeder, making sure his work would pass the inspection of old Scarbreath himself, Brown the Fourth, Point Six. Brownie 46, as Jack and the other farmhands were wont to call the mutant overseer, had a total anal-retentive mania about straight "agro-rows," as he called them. Nonetheless, Jack Bender found himself having a very difficult time keeping the row straight.

He kept on thinking about what he'd seen.

The plane had disappeared off into the area that Jack knew very well. In fact, it was the place where he kept his secret shack—the one space in this world that was Jack's, and Jack's alone. That area was still undeveloped, but it was within the periphery that Jack was allowed to roam without one of the implants embedded in his body going off in Central Agro-Control and bringing out the goon squad to paddle his butt or laminate his brain back into "functional" order. Good farmies, after all, just had absolutely no reason to roam. They did their jobs, they sang their songs, they read their approved books, they watched their approved shows, they made love, and they ate their good old-fashioned home cooking.

Just like the good slaves that they were.

They were not called slaves, of course. The complex called them one of their "human communes."

11

They were a big, generally happy family, and Jack Bender, at the age of twenty, had no real reason to complain. He had a girlfriend, he had work, he had friends, he knew who he was . . . When some of his group whispered in the corners about the Human Liberation Front and the glories of freedom and individuality, the lost state of liberty, Jack Bender got far, far away. He knew which side his corncob was buttered on, and that's just what he'd told Phil Potts, his friend who was fascinated by the legends of the freedom fighters that somehow filtered through the complex's dampers.

"Yeah, and you know why they butter it, don't you!" Phil had said. "So they can ram it up your ass!"

Such rebellious talk bothered Jack, but he tuned it out. However, much as he would have liked to, he could not tune out thinking about that plane he thought he'd seen. For one thing, Jack was fascinated with flying. About all he could hope to fly were models and kites, but he longed to soar free above the ground—he dreamed of the experience often. For another thing, that plane—if it was a plane—had been coming down at an awfully steep angle. True, there had been no crashing sounds, no explosion, and no column of smoke rising up beyond the trees. But that didn't mean that whoever was in the plane couldn't be hurt, couldn't need help.

That last realization was the clincher.

Jack Bender was the compassionate type. The thought that someone might be in trouble, might be hurt, might need his help, made him realize he had a duty to check it out. Of course, he could always just notify the authorities. The complex would send out a crew of mutie Searcher units to check out the situation. Somehow, though, deep in his gut, Jack didn't think this was a good idea.

Searchers didn't exactly have a reputation for being gentle, and often as not the humans they went out looking for came back in a box stamped RESEARCH.

Right. Decision made.

As Jack looked out to the vast stretch of unseeded field, he knew that it would take hours to finish, hours before he got a chance to go and take a look—and such were the limitations of farmboy life that the muties kept pretty close tabs on their hands.

Ping, said the chugging seed-machine. *Ping.*

Jack Bender looked down at the casing of the engine, and a little grin plucked up the corners of his mouth.

"Tomorrow!" said Brown the Fourth, Point Six. "Boy, you've got the whole south forty to seed by the weekend, and you say you're not going to be able to get the right part for this thing until *tomorrow!"* Brown 46 scratched at the side of his neck the way he did when he got irritated. Dead scales fluttered down onto the mutant's jacket and onto the garage floor. Brown was an Upper Quadrant Post-Human: he had brains, his breed specifically gene-spliced for business management. His training had been pure agro, and Jack supposed he was pretty good at it. The problem with Brownie was that, like most mutants, he was very linear. He had a real problem dealing with mishaps and changes of plans.

Also, he could be a real asshole too. Like now.

"Look, we have to face reality, sir," said Jack, his smooth-complexioned, square-jawed face all smiles and conciliation. "I'll tell you what, though. I'll work

13

the weekend. I'll have all my plots seeded by the time the inspector comes around.''

Brown 46 scratched some more. Brown 46 shed more scales. Of course, Brown 46 had plenty of scales to spare—his whole body was covered with them, looking like the heartbreak of psoriasis gone terminal. The manager was bald too, with no ears, slanty eyes and a stubby nose, hardly any chin—all of which gave his head the look of a silly, unsinister snake forever laying its eggs. A kind of musky smell hung over him, like sour sweat, but Jack was used to the smell. All mutants smelled weird to humans. But then, all humans smelled *bad* to mutants, which was just one more item to add to the list of why mutants *hated* humans.

"I don't know . . . maybe I should send you out on one of the spares," Brown said in his high, gurgling voice.

Jack shook his head adamantly. "Sir, with all due respect, that would be really du— I mean, it just wouldn't work. I've worked on the spares. Most of the spares have been cannibalized for parts for the other machines."

Brown blinked. "You can't get your part from one of the spares that way?"

Jack looked down at the oily parts of the seeder, strewn along a drop cloth, trying hard to look as though he was taking the suggestion seriously. "No, I'm afraid not. That particular cam is peculiar to this model, and I'm just going to have to go into Central this evening when the hardware annex opens for farmies and get the exact kind I need—the kind I know will make it through the week . . . So the job can get done and we'll all look good when the inspector comes next week."

The agromanager couldn't argue with that, not really, but he had to go through his mutie war dance to save his self-respect. "You're a foul incompetent, creature, subhuman."

"Yes, sir."

"I should string you up and beat you."

"I would deserve it, sir."

Brown 46 raised a leathery hand as though about to strike, and Jack Bender cringed. But Brown shrugged, as he did as often as not, and satisfied himself with spitting a gob of green-streaked phlegm on Jack's workboots. "Just don't forget your promise, subbie."

"No, sir, I won't."

Face saved (and what an ugly one, thought Jack), Brown 46 swiveled around and minced away back toward his office to return to his piddling paperwork or agroplans or whatever.

Jack grinned.

Yes, exactly as he expected. Brown might be a decent manager to his mutie inspectors, but he had about as much imagination as a snail. He didn't think about assigning Jack another job for the morning and afternoon. It would be lunchtime before the thought would worm its way into the mutie's thick skull, and by then Jack would be back and happy to oblige.

He had all morning to roam as he liked—as long as it was within the farm periphery. Absently, Jack fingered the small scar at his throat, where the tracer implant had been placed. One of his few uneasy feelings here on the farm was about that implant—and maybe about the even smaller scars from the scrapings. After years of the tiny operations, Bender's body was absolutely riddled with tiny scars, just like everyone else on the work farms or factories where humans

15

were kept. Jack was never sure of the exact reason for these small operations. There was that bogeyman story from his childhood that said that the mutant Overlords used the extractions for tasty midnight snacks. But Phil Potts, who'd somehow smuggled illegal books into his own private place in the dorm cellar, claimed that what the mutants were after was "fresh genetic material" with which to experiment, and probably to renew their own DNA supplies in their breeder vats.

It was all a bit beyond Jack Bender, who was basically a happy-go-lucky kind of guy.

He waited until he knew Brown 46 was far away, and then he quietly sneaked out of the mechanics' barn unit of the complex. All of his fellows would be hard at work now at their respective tasks; he could easily head back out to the forest unobserved.

Jack Bender knew this because he'd done it before.

He was skirting the dairy complex, passing through the rich smell of sour milk and sour cows, when he bumped into the last person he wanted to see. Last *human,* anyway. Phil Potts.

"Bender," said Potts.

"Potts," said Bender, trying to walk by.

Potts wouldn't let it go at that. He grabbed Bender by his red flannel workshirt, in the brusque but unthreatening manner that was all Phil Potts, frustrated revolutionary.

"Hey, wait. We need to talk."

"Phil, I can't. I really need—"

Potts looked about in his usual paranoid are-there-any-muties-around horizon sweep. He was a short, intense guy with dark eyes and a Roman nose. His hair was long, although Brown 46 kept making him cut it. Somehow, this time he'd gotten the length of

16

his blond locks over his ears. "This won't take long. You hear about Montero?"

"Bill Montero? What about him?"

"Didn't show up in his dorm last night. Nowhere to be seen today." Potts's teeth were clenched, his neck muscles rigid. "I knew Montero. No way did he want to go over the hill. He was like you, Bender. He *liked* it here."

"So? Maybe he went to see an aunt in the Dubuque Shoe Factory. Now, Potts, I got something important to—"

"That's the second one this month. Third in three months. I'm telling you, Bender, something fishy's going on. And the weird thing is, the muties—they honestly seem to be baffled about it."

Bender shrugged. It was his turn to frown, a little grim. "Maybe it's natural selection time." To wit: a mutant weeding out of bad stock. This was where Jack Bender got into cringe time, and the full nastiness of the slave system got shoved in his face. This was when it was hard to ignore the truth about not only the metaphorical chains that hung about his neck, but the faint whiff of horror that hung over this farm.

"What? Williams was a prize specimen. Ever see the pecs and delts on that guy? Incredible. And no dummy, either. And Lisa Nulty? Whew! They had her all pegged as prime breeding stock."

"Look, I'm sorry to hear about Montero. And I'll keep my eyes and ears open, Phil, I promise. But I gotta go, really."

Potts nodded, releasing the flannel. "One of these days you're gonna realize that we can't take this much longer, Bender. One of these days you're gonna realize that I've been right all along. I need you, man. I can see that you've got the most potential of all the

17

whole thousand human souls in this complex. We can do it, man, we can break *outta* here, join the freedom fighters.''

"Yeah," snorted Bender. "And have the lifespan of a fly at crop dusting time!''

Potts's eyes grew wide and wild and yearning. "But at least we'll be *free*, Jack. *Free!* Like humans are supposed to be."

"You know me, Potts. I like flush toilets, TV, and regular meals. Bye."

"Yes, I know you, Bender," said Potts as Jack strolled away. "But do you really know yourself?"

Jack put as much distance as possible, as quickly as possible, between him and Potts. He didn't like to hang around with the guy, and he certainly didn't want the muties to see him in Potts's company—not now, anyway. With that kind of talk, and his collection of contraband literature, Phillip Potts was headed for a major fall, sure as shooting, and Jack did not want to get dragged down with him.

Maybe he was right though, the niggling little thought crept into his head. Maybe humans weren't meant for this kind of treatment. Goodness knew, it pissed Bender off something royal the way he had to kowtow sometimes. And the stories he'd heard about mutant atrocities during the War and afterward . . . The atrocities he heard whispered about now . . .

But the hard truth also was that Jack Bender *enjoyed* most of the life he had here. He liked hard work, and Brownie put enough responsibilities on his shoulders to make him feel important, and part of a functioning group. And he liked Jenny, his girlfriend, too, lots and lots . . . But he felt pretty smug and satisfied that if Jenny and he stopped seeing each other, what with his strapping, tousled good looks and his hard, slender body, he'd probably find another girlfriend fairly quick. And boy, he had plenty of lookers here to choose from . . . if he could just get his act together. Being on a work farm in Iowa had its advantages. The ladies, with their corn-fed complexions and figures and their Scandinavian-touched beauty, were *wonderful*.

And high on Jack Bender's list of weaknesses was beautiful women.

Now, if he could only figure out how to talk to them right.

Jenny had pretty much just kind of lassoed him last year; he hadn't done any work. And since theirs had been a steady relationship, he'd gotten out of practice with women. Oh, he caught some looking at him now and again, but whenever he tried to talk to them (behind Jenny's back, of course) he got all tongue-tied and stupid.

Oh well, he thought. There were other more important things to contemplate right now. And more important things to *do!*

Making sure no one was watching him, he struck off from the last building in the complex and headed out for the fields and trees where he had seen the plane descending.

CHAPTER 2

In a chamber deep below a Colorado mountain where once a nation called the United States of America had kept the headquarters for its watchdog system known as NORAD, a cyborg screamed.

The mighty tenor howl, trebling occasionally with ululations, throbbed through the wires with the power of maximum voltage, echoing through the steel and glass subterranean chambers of the nerve center, was a sound not unfamiliar to the many breeds of mutants working in the DeepZone Ganglia. Nonetheless, none of them ever got used to it, especially the technician breed who had to clean up the havoc it caused in the computers and the machines.

When the Overlord screamed, it meant not only that he was upset, angry, displeased, what-have-you.

It meant that heads were going to roll.

"What do you mean, he *escaped!*" said His Supremacy, Overlord and Master of the Upper Americas, Emperor Ignatius Charlemagne the Seventh, Point Five.

The BrainGeneral stood before the dais at attention, his face a mask of stoicism. "Maximillian Turkel's guerrilla attack on the Kansas air base punched out their radar system. No pilots were immediately on hand to man pursuit in the undestroyed light planes.

However, I am happy to say, Your Highness, that we know for a fact that his plane was headed north. As we have very good reason to believe that the hellspawn traitor to the True Cause was wounded, we believe him to have gotten no farther than the Iowa Provinces. May it please Your Lord, we have dispatched a Bloodhound squadron and have organized an aerial reconnaissance of that area specifically to ferret out Turkel."

The Overlord grew silent, his great bulk slowly settling from its roiling fury.

Somehow, the effect was more terrifying than the screaming. His minions, his technicians, his physicians, and his chiropractors stood a step farther back to make sure they were out of reach of the spike-studded, jewel-encrusted leather bands wrapped around his meaty wrists; his arms had a tendency to flail at moments of high drama, and more than one attendant had lost an eye or suffered a punctured lung in the process.

Overlord Charlemagne 75 was of a mutant race specifically bred by the BrainGenerals for certain capacities. To rule, to organize, and, most importantly, to plug into the extensive computer and telecommunications arrays, much of their extensive brains functioning as a kind of neocortex for the vast artificial intelligence of the computer systems the mutant races had inherited from their human predecessors. Even now, the Overlord was interfaced, one quarter of his body plugged directly into the exposed control-node conduits and chips of the megacomputer via cybercables glistening wetly like exposed nerves. An occasional spark shivered along their twisting color-coded lengths: pure thought wrangling with pure electricity.

21

Thus, the Overlord looked like an immensely fat man being swallowed by a large metallic snake.

The Overlords had been bred to be over eight feet tall, with very little muscle and much skin. Although they had not all been bald, Charlemagne was, his sweaty skin a vivid mottling of purple and red below the muted lights on the vaulted ceiling. Occasional gobs of skin poked through a massive golden robe that hung on his immensity like a rich man's tent. However, obese as the Emperor seemed, much of his girth did not consist of fat. It was gray matter. Brainstuff, unconfined by a skull, lodged insecurely beneath mere skin. Indeed, if one looked closely at one of the larger protuberant masses moving beneath, say, one of the Overlord's chins like a gigantic goiter, or on that protruded from his abdomen like an immense cancer, one would see beneath the veiny translucent skin the telltale convolutions of mutant brainstuff.

With such genetic technology as this had the mutants, created to serve humanity, enslaved their masters.

Their creators, however, had never dreamed that this would be possible.

After the Great Powers of the world realized that use of nuclear weapons in conflict would be mutually catastrophic, and the pickings for the winning side would be entirely radioactive and useless, final multilateral disarmament was finally achieved by the year 2010. Even the smaller nuclear powers such as Pakistan and Israel claimed to have divested themselves of their fierce and terrible weapons. There were those who doubted this; nonetheless, no nuclear weapons were ever used afterward.

However, nations still existed, and so did war. Previous peace between the United States and the Soviet

Union and most particularly between the Soviet Union and China was undermined. Conflict began. New nonnuclear weapons to fight this war were needed.

These weapons were found in the first batch of vat-bred beings formed of human germ plasm and specifically bred for infantry battle.

Mutants.

It was South Africa that pointed the way to hell.

In 2005, the University of Johannesburg announced its success in genetically altering certain species of animals. Using advanced laser technology and sophisticated electron microscopes, the very stuff of life—the chains of life, DNA, and its coils of amino acids—could be cut and reinserted like a child's set of Tinker Toys. Cows were altered to provide larger quantities of milk or beef. Chickens laid bigger eggs, and South African guard dogs got suspiciously bigger and nastier.

However, what the University of Johannesburg did not announce was that this forging ahead in biotechnology was financed by the racist government for specific reasons.

When the Great South African Rebellion finally came in 2017 and hundreds of thousands of oppressed blacks finally tried to overthrow the white authors of apartheid, the government unleashed its secret weapon on the masses.

Genetically bred fighting machines.

Humanoid, these creatures, though of a very low intelligence, were like creatures from hell on the streets. Experts with both weapons and their tungsten-reinforced claws and metal-banded teeth, they ripped through crowds like buzzsaws. And for every one of these monstrosities brought down, another seemed to take its place. After a hundred thousand blacks were horribly massacred in less than three days, the mere mention of these fighting machines on legs caused whole villages to stampede in screaming fear. The Rebellion ended with whites the affirmed masters once more. But though the appearance of mutant fighters in South Africa preserved the status quo in South Africa, they not only changed the world, they altered the course of history irrevocably.

Intelligence efforts increased. Secrets were bought from traitors. Within two years, mutant fighting creatures appeared in Third World countries. South Africa became rich manufacturing them and selling them, certainly, but since it could not hang on to its scientific secrets for long, soon all the major powers knew how to manufacture the monstrous terrors. And though the Soviet Union and most particularly the United States publicly decried the use of these twisted parodies of human soldiers, secretly they created their own versions themselves.

All in the interest of national security.

Soon, it was the Cold War all over again, countries vying for secrets, countries breeding newer and deadlier species of mutants. But this new Cold War had a deadly twist: there was no nuclear deterrent. Limited warfare was possible. And though the stronger powers somehow held themselves in check for a time, they funneled their conventional weaponry (developed to new heights of technical sophistication) to puppet states, along with the mutant warriors. These specially bred creatures became the new frontline soldiers.

Although the first of these surrogate berserkers were very low-level in intelligence, the "mutant gap" and the need for specialized breeds to operate the more difficult equipment of war led to higher mutant IQ levels.

So by the time the World War broke out, many of the mutants were very intelligent indeed . . .

The Emperor broke his silence, his high-pitched, grating voice vibrating about the chamber like the squeals of a trapped rodent.

"Are you aware, BrainGeneral Torx, of the trouble that this subhuman Maximillian Turkel has caused? Are you acquainted at all with the havoc he has stirred into the Effort, to say nothing of the severe rocking he has given the Sacred Equilibrium of the North Americas?"

BrainGeneral Torx raised bushy eyebrows, but otherwise his broad, twisted features remained expressively inert. But for the disfigured face, he might well have been a normal-looking human being, not a vatborn creature at all.

"Yes, my Lord. I assumed he was sufficiently important to warrant my exclusive attention."

The vast, glutinous surface of the Overlord's skin began to wobble and tremble like a quivery mass of molded gelatin. His eyes widened and glowed with hatred and frustration. "Exclusive attention! If he had your exclusive attention, why was this raid upon our sacred air base possible? And why were you not even *there* to pursue him properly?"

BrainGeneral Torx's eyes tilted down to the brightly polished floor. "He tricked me, Your Lordship. My intelligence had it that the attack was to be in Oklahoma Province, not Kansas. He must have planted that information with my spies on purpose."

The Overlord shook. "You see! You see, Brain-General! I warned you last month! The man is the archdevil himself! Subhumans, of course, do not have anywhere near the intelligence of we high life forms—but by the Sacred Vat, they can be well equipped with infernal cunning.'' The Overlord ground his teeth, and his eyes bugged so far from their sockets that they looked like bloodshot marbles about to pop out and roll away. ''This Turkel has been tormenting me for over twenty years now! Each time we catch him, he somehow escapes! The so-called freedom fighters he rallies and leads have grown in number. BrainGeneral Torx, you well know that the Effort has more important tasks ahead of it than quelling mutiny among our *slaves!*''

''Yes, my Lord. I well know.''

''Then how do you explain your impotence in this matter!''

A flash of expression crossed Torx's face. The eyes showed a glimmer of anger and outrage, the spark of rebellion, the glimpse of an intelligent creature who has had to work beneath unthinkable arrogance and malevolence for far too long. ''My Lord, the problem is that we have underestimated the abilities of the humans. But more than that, my Lord, *you* do not seem to understand the hunger in their breasts for freedom from their yokes. *This* is what makes a man like Max Turkel so desperate, so smart, so cunning. He is willing to risk his life, yea, even his very soul for the taste of liberty—and for liberty for his kind!''

A wave of crimson apoplexy passed over the fat mottled face of Overlord Charlemagne. Sparks arced and spat across the periphery of his cyberattachment tubing. ''What!'' he said, specks of drool spraying and dripping from his grouperlike mouth. ''What did you say, BrainGeneral! Blasphemy! The creatures are

26

nothing more than *subhuman!* We are the true humanity! We are the Trueborn! We—''

Such was the Overlord's rage that his gross form began to shake and contort. He bent toward the BrainGeneral as though to grab him by his throat, forgetting that his stubby Thalidomide-baby flapper feet were incapable of walking.

There was an audible *snap!* that echoed round the room.

The Overlord froze, his face a mask of pain. All color left it, and suddenly the creature was as pale as a ghost.

''My back!'' he gasped. ''Oh! My back!''

Overlord Charlemagne hung listing to the side, canted at an absurd angle, kept from falling onto the floor of the dais only by the cybercables connecting him to the computer.

After a moment of stunned stares, his physicians and attendants went to work. Utilizing a collection of scaffolding machines, they shored their master up, easing some of the pressure. However, they could not put the Overlord into place; his back had gone out.

This was a job for the Royal Chiropractors.

Chiropractor mutants were a race of weasely-looking humanoids with growths resembling mustaches, that were actually fungal in nature, beneath large noses. They had poor eyesight and so tended to wear large round glasses that made their pupil-less eyes look like those of deep-sea fish. Because of the large amount of oil their skins exuded, their dark limp hair tended to be pasted against their heads greasily. The collective philosophy of the breed was that since spines ultimately connected with every nerve in the body, to say nothing of its owner's pocketbook, manipulation of said spine would produce not merely an

27

easing of pain but weight loss around the wallet area. Their guild had convinced the Overlord that he need chiropractic attention; now was the time that they would prove their value.

Bogg Putz, DMC, the head mutant Chiropractor, directed his associates to bring around the equipment and immediately set to work, his pale eyes ludicrously large in the lenses of his glasses. He scrambled about issuing directions, and once all his contraptions were properly arranged, he cracked his long fingers, climbed up a ladder, and proceeded to place a kind of half nelson on his patient's neck.

The mutant Chiropractor twisted once, hard.

The popping sound was like the crack of a bat connecting with a home run.

"All right, Your Highness!" said Bogg Putz. "You are healed!"

The Overlord opened his mouth, but instead of a "thank you," a horrible howl issued forth, filling the chamber with pain and fury.

"Fool! What . . . what did you . . . do!"

Bogg Putz, DMC, blinked. "My Lord! A simple subluxation of your lumbar—"

"It's *worse!* You want subluxation, I'll give you subluxation!"

A cybercoil in the array connecting the Overlord twisted, glowing a bright orange. As though in immediate reaction, a clanking *thud* sounded from beyond a portal. All heads turned as the creaking and thudding continued: footsteps. Suddenly, a hulking metallic form filled the portal, blocking out the light. It squeezed through, and then pounded forward, slowly but surely, toward the dais.

A robot.

One of the Overlord's technobots actually, operated

by Charlemagne's mental commands. Servomechanisms encased in duroplastic glowed and worked like the intricate interior of a clock. The monstrous thing stomped forward.

When the head mutant Chiropractor realized what was happening, he panicked. He jumped down the ladder and tried to scurry away. However, one of the robot's arm's extended with a whir, clamping onto the rodentlike creature, and bringing him to an abrupt halt.

"Now, fool," said the Overlord, his eyes beginning to glitter with pleasure. "I make a little venture into your field of medicine myself."

The robot pulled the squirming, screaming mutant up a full five feet into the air. Servoclamps connected around his chest cavity, holding him fast as the other arm swung around, its hand changing and rearranging form even as it moved.

Suddenly, the robot hand was a pair of sharp-nosed pliers.

With a motion as swift as a striking adder, these pliers stabbed into the base of the mutant's back.

There was a snapping sound.

The mutant screamed.

Slowly and carefully, like a man deveining a shrimp, the robot pulled the mutant's spine from his back, clipping off the ribs with auxiliary shears along the way.

The mutant struggled and screamed for a short time before it died, streaming a rain of blood onto the polished floor. Then, with one final spasm, it hung limply in the metal embrace of its killer.

When the robot had the spine bared all the way up to the neck, it used its razor shears to cut off the head entirely.

29

The body flopped onto the floor like a discarded dummy. However, the extracted spine still hung in the robot's hand, attached to the mutant's severed head.

The hush of horror that had swept the room with the violent demise of the mutant Chiropractor gave way now to whispers and gasps as the robot swiveled around to face BrainGeneral Torx. Its servomotors hissed and its joints squeaked as it walked toward the mutant commander, dripping a gory record of its path.

Torx stood straight, staring off past the approaching monstrosity, steeling himself for whatever might happen next. It was not his style to attempt to flee; besides, such a course of action was silly. There was no escape from these underground rooms, operated entirely on the whim of the cybermutant Overlord.

If it was death he faced, then so be it. BrainGeneral Torx had stared death in the face before without blinking.

The robot clanked to a halt before him.

"Torx!" cried Overlord Charlemagne.

"Yes, my Lord."

"BrainGeneral Torx! Catch!"

The robot tossed the grisly remnant of the Royal Chiropractor to the BrainGeneral. Torx caught it by the head. The mouth and the eyes were wide open, frozen in pain and horror.

"Regard well the handiwork of the metal at my command!" squeaked the Overlord. "Catch the rebel Maximillian Turkel. Catch him and bring him here to my fortress, dead or alive, by the end of a lunar cycle—or the fate that you hold in your hands will be your own!"

BrainGeneral Torx said nothing.

"Do you understand, BrainGeneral?"

"Yes, my Lord."

"And BrainGeneral. I shall take my *time* about it with you. You are in the Sacred Trust. Do not abuse your privilege." He cleared his throat, and his eyes swept over the assembled quivering attendants and physicians from their absurdly canted position. "Now then. Get me a decent osteopath!"

The attendants raced away to obey the command.

CHAPTER 3

Jack Bender entered the trees.

You couldn't call it a forest, not really. These were a lot of trees for Iowa, but they didn't exactly call for attention by a forest ranger. How they had escaped the axes of the mutants nobody every really knew—the new rulers of the land had the reputation of razing all trees in the interest of maximum agronomic return from the still rich and fecund bread-basket soil. However, they'd spared this patch of firs and elms and whatever other kinds of trees (Jack was always promising himself to look up their exact names in one of Phil Potts's textbooks, but somehow he never quite got around to it).

He was trying to remember exactly over the tops of what trees he thought he'd seen the plane drop.

That was difficult to determine, since he'd been in the field about a mile away at the time, and his sense of direction had gotten rather discombobulated.

Oh, well, he thought. He had time to make a thorough look. The woods were simply not all that big.

The smell of spring pine and the wildflowers laced the air pleasantly. They were relaxing, familiar smells, yet wonderful and new every time he experienced them, along with the dozens of other bracing sensations he felt when walking among the trees. This was something he did often, when he had the time, when he didn't feel like hanging out at his private place he'd built a little further back, or like hanging around at the complex with his fellow humans or the mutants. A guy could just sort of drift out here of a morning, unshackle his soul, and fly it like a kite in the air, free and glorious as a bird. Yes, if he didn't have this kind of experience to fall back on, maybe he would try and go "over the fence" with Phil Potts. But that simply wasn't the case. Jack Bender felt as though he had everything, just about everything, a guy should want here on the farm compound, even the occasional illusion of freedom. Why should he want to give it all up?

A bird twittered in the branches above him. A squirrel scurried up a tree. The trees seemed alive and vibrant with a spring breeze and they fairly shook with vitality to the music of its fluting past bark and leaves.

Besides, thought Jack Bender, freedom is overrated anyway. Nobody is free, not really. What a human being had, at the end of it all, was just death and nothingness. So why not just enjoy the important stuff in life—food, music, sex, hard satisfying work— avoiding as much of the ample pain available as possible.

Still, though, a thought nagged at him. It *would* be nice to be able to go out into the trees and fields, go fishing, go hunting, whatever, whenever he pleased. Sure, he was pretty good at sneaking out like this . . .

But still, it would be nice to go of his own free will . . .

Free will . . .

The phrase echoed in his mind like a tune you can't get out of your head.

Phil Potts used it a lot, along with gallons of other gloppy talk, and generally Jack tried to ignore the words. He didn't have much use for philosophy. He was too busy either *doing* or *not doing,* he'd told Potts once. The guy had only laughed and suggested that maybe that was a pretty profound philosophy as well.

Jack didn't get the joke.

He'd been searching for a little under a half hour when he came across the snapped tree. Branches were littered across the ground, and Jack could see a swath, cut by something through the trees, angling down toward a clearing beyond.

Yep. It had been a plane all right.

Jack Bender hurried along. Whoever was in the plane could be needing help, bad.

He found the small crashed plane at the other side of a clearing maybe fifty, sixty yards wide. The pilot would have had to be in control and a good pilot to put a plane down in such a small space; still, the small thing had tipped over, one of its wings crumpled. It wasn't burned, though, which was a good sign, although Jack could smell the telltale fumes of gasoline as he approached it.

Carefully, he checked the cockpit. There was no one inside, but there was blood there, a lot of it. The door was open; the pilot had crawled out. Jack followed the drips of blood into the trees.

He found the pilot past a stand of bushes.

The man lay propped against a tree, unconscious, covered with blood. However, he was still alive; Jack could see his chest rising and falling regularly.

He was a big guy, the fallen pilot—large chest, big shoulders, two days' growth of beard around a lantern jaw, and large fierce eyebrows atop a darkly handsome face. There were several wounds, in his chest

34

and his leg and along his arm, red and wet with blood. Jack had a curious feeling that he had seen the man's face before. He got a strange sensation tingling along his spine—this was, somehow, a very *important* meeting.

Certainly it was for the pilot. The man needed help, and badly.

When Jack was about ten feet away, the man's eyes opened and fixed on him.

"Hey there, dude," he said in a deep, resonant, if weary voice. "You wanna stop where you are. I got this gun in my pocket, you see, and I'd like to make sure you're not a goddamned mutie."

Jack grinned. "Yeah, right. Can't you see my webbed ears and nose!" This guy might be bleeding, but he didn't look like he was going to give up any time real soon. "Seriously, I'm a friend. I want to help if I can."

The man realized noticeably. "Help? Who, me? Shit, kid, I'm in great shape. I don't need no help. Maybe a pint or two of blood, that's all, and a new body might help."

Jack approached. Up closer, he could better see the extent of the man's damage. And it didn't look good.

"Gee, mister. You look like Swiss cheese."

"Kee-rist, fella, it's not that bad. And hell, if it is, I sure as hell don't want to *hear* about it."

"Sorry. What can I do?"

"Well, for starters, I can tell you that there are some goons looking for me, so if you want to help the cause of human liberation and free school lunches, maybe we better get me hidden someplace. Maybe then I'll live long enough to heal."

"Human liber— gosh."

"Say shit or damn, kid, or you'll make me wish they'd caught me."

"Uhm . . . yeah . . . Shit! Uh, yeah . . . Fuck! You see, I can say those words too . . . It's just that the muties, well, they tend to clean out our mouths with soap."

"Yeah, one more reason to blow the motherkillers to hell. So what's your name, kid?"

"Jack, sir. Jack Bender."

"Yeah, good to meet you, Jack. I'm Max Turkel. Now, you wanna start thinkin' about where you're gonna take me, and like maybe start *acting* on it?"

"Oh, yeah, right. Can you walk?"

"Yes. I'm just a little bit weak. Legs are okay though."

"Can you climb? With help I mean?"

"Climb? Have I fallen in the hands of a crazed drill instructor?"

"No. I've got a tree house. I can put you there."

"Christ, what is this, Tarzan of the Apes?"

Jack grinned. If this guy could crack jokes, then he still had enough blood in him to live awhile longer. "Yeah, and I guess that makes you Jane, huh?"

"Shit, no. Fuckin' Cheetah. The way we flubbed that last hit, you would've thought we had the brains of chimpanzees or something."

"Hit?" said Jack, bending over the man and figuring out the best way to lift him up.

"Yeah. A mutie air force base in Kansas. We were blowing it to hell before a bunch of mutants I ain't never seen before came charging up from bomb shelters. Must've been in stasis, waitin' for just such a situation. Christ, I gotta save my breath." He reached out tentatively with a bloody arm. "Take me to your tree hut, Tarz. And please be gentle."

* * *

The man who had called himself Max Turkel was a big man, heavy and muscular. It was tough to take him the three-quarters of a mile to where Jack had built his tree fort years ago. Still, for all the blood he'd lost and the way he looked as though he was going to faint from time to time, the man hung in there gamely and bravely. Jack took it real careful though; he didn't want the man to start bleeding bad again. Maybe he could deal with the wounds the guy had now, with the help of some of Phil Potts's surgery books and some supplies he could filch from the MedCenter. But no way could he stop heavy bleeding with what he had in the hut.

"Here we are," Jack said.

"I don't see anything."

"That's the idea." Jack pointed up to the wealth of branches and leaves. "It's up there. Foilage isn't much good in the winter, but I'm not about to come out here in the snow anyway, and neither are the muties."

Turkel grinned weakly. "Yeah. Fuckers don't like the chill, do they?"

"No sirree bob. I mean, fuckin' no way, Mr. Turkel—"

"Max, kid. Call me Max."

"Anyway, it's up there, Max."

"Yeah. Right. Maybe you'd better set me down for a spell. Let me rest a bit before we start climbing Mount Everest, huh."

"Okay. How about that batch of shade over there. Mist— I mean, Max."

"That shade looks real good, kid."

Jack took him over behind the thick bole of the oak that supported his tree fort and carefully helped him

37

to lie down. Apparently, the bleeding had not started up bad again, and Max Turkel was still hanging tenaciously on to his consciousness.

He was a big guy all right, Turkel, with a shock of black hair and heavy eyebrows and dark brooding eyes that nonetheless looked capable of holding a few twinkles to them if the man was in the mood. His nose was bent, many times broken, and as Max put him down, he noticed all the scars the man had on his face, neck, and bare muscular arms.

Every bit of this man spelled *warrior.*

"Yeah. Oooh. Okay. I think I got a busted rib, that's about all. And somehow those bullets missed vital plumbing."

"Gee—those slashes. How'd you get those?"

"You don't want to know, kid. You'll get nightmares."

"You just want to sit here while I go and get some medical stuff to patch you up with?"

"Nah, get my butt up in your tree house first. I can make it, just let this perforated carcass get some air in its bags first. Say, you must be a farm kid or something."

"That's right."

"Slave on a compound, huh?"

"A worker, Max. Neither we nor the Comrade Workers use that word."

"Yeah, right. Like you fucking call a crapper a WC, huh? Like you call forced buggery a rear sexual assault. You're a fucking slave, pal, just like I was. I can see the control node in your neck. They got you penned in here like a dog."

Jack Bender's eyes flashed. "You know, I could just let your bones rot right here, you asshole!"

Turkel grinned. "Hey! The farmboy's got a vocabulary after all.'' Weakly, Turkel patted Jack's arm. ''Just tryin' to get a rise out of you, boy. You got some stuff, I can tell. Maybe I got myself a recruit for the movement, huh?''

''The only movements I get involved with are the ones I do in the crapper, Max.''

''Yeah, yeah. Okay. Sorry. Maybe I hit a delicate subject. But hell, you're helping me, aren't you?''

''You need help. I don't want you to die. After that . . .''

Those large heavy eyebrows lowered. ''You're not going to tell the muties, are you, son?''

It was Jack's turn to grin mischievously. ''Just tryin' to get a rise out of you, old man.''

Those deep dark eyes glittered with sudden good humor. ''Motherfucker. I pray for salvation and the devil himself answers. I get the feeling that with you the muties pay dearly for their cheap labor, huh, kid?''

Jack just smiled mischievously.

He looked up at the dark hold of the trees, calculating.

''Look, Max. You think you can climb a rope ladder, or shall I just have to figure on some other way of getting you up?''

''You bring one of your corn-fed girlfriends out here, buddy, you'll get me up!''

''Seriously.''

''Okay. Seriously. Yeah, I've climbed a few rope ladders in worse condition than this. Right. Just give me a couple more minutes.''

''You got it.'' Jack went to the base of the tree and began to dig.

''Buried treasure?'' inquired Max.

''Nope.'' Jack pulled out climbing pitons, brushed off dirt, and tied them onto his ankles. ''Way I figure it, I got a ladder, it's just one more chance of the muties finding out my little secret. This place, it's important to me. I don't want that."

So saying, he climbed up the bark the twenty feet to the first branch.

"Jesus *Christ!*" said Max Turkel, flopping over onto the wooden platform fronting the door of Jack Bender's tree house with the help of Jack's hands. "How high up is this mother?"

"High enough. I'm impressed, Max. You got *some* guts."

"Yeah, and I think I left a few back there hanging on the branches. Pardon me while I expire."

Jack checked the wounds. Fresh blood. Shit, maybe he shouldn't have made the guy climb. But it wasn't much blood, and sure as hell the guy was a hell of a lot safer up here in Hog Heaven than down there on the ground.

That was what Jack called this place, Hog Heaven. It was a simple enough structure of wood and nails and shingles, but it kept the rain out and it was big enough inside not to get claustrophic or anything.

Jack helped Turkel through the door and put him on one of the mats atop the rough pine floor. Then he went over to one of his makeshift cabinets. "You want some water, Max?"

"You bet I do. My fucking mouth feels like the Mojave in dry season."

Jack handed him a canteen and Max drank thirstily, then fell back onto the mat. "Whew. Thanks, kid. I don't suppose you got something a little stronger than water to keep me company while you go get those medical supplies."

"Well, Hank Sayers—he's a friend of mine in agrochem—he's kinda old and grizzled and he has this still in the back of the lab. Gave me some 'corn whiskey,' he calls it, last year, and me and my girl, Jenny, we got *real* sick on it.''

''Sounds good to me. Got any left?''

''Yeah. I think so. But do you think it's a good idea . . . I mean, in your condition.''

''Don't worry, kid. I never met a jar of home liquor that didn't like me.''

''I'll get it.'' Jack went back to his cabinets. These were well stocked with canned goods and bottles as well as a few books, old dogeared girlie magazines, and a rats' nest of stuff from his boyhood he'd half forgotten: slingshots, balls, bats, jacks, marbles, dead insects, what-have-you. Jack rooted around in the mess, looking for that bottle of booze.

''I don't suppose you have any cigarettes, do you?''

''Muties look at tobacco same way as alcohol. Forbidden stuff. Kills off the workers.''

''Then I assume you've got some, and I'm sure that they won't mind if I smoke.''

Jack nodded. ''No, I don't suppose they *would* mind.'' He found his packet of hand-rolled numbers, and then almost immediately spotted the half-full beaker of clear potent whiskey. It was stoppered with a cork. ''You're in luck on both counts.'' He brought Turkel the cigarettes and the whiskey. Then he got a cup and a box of matches.

He had to admit that as soon as Max Turkel was blowing some smoke and had killed a couple of fingers of whiskey, he actually looked as though he might live.

''Yeah,'' said Turkel. ''Thanks.''

''I'll go get that stuff now.''

"Sure." When Jack reached the door, Turkel called to him. "Hey, kid."

"Yes."

In the dimness of the kerosene lamp that Jack had lit, the farmboy could see Max Turkel's eyes, deep and serious.

"I owe you, kid. I think I got myself a new pal."

An odd stirring touched Jack inside.

"Just don't drink too much, pass out, and burn my tree house down."

Turkel smiled weakly.

CHAPTER 4

BrainGeneral Mordechai Torx the Fifth, Point Nine, was not a happy mutant.

"Bring me one of the prisoners," he snapped harshly, pacing his office. "The strongest human available, the quickest of reflex, the best fighter. My honor demands amelioration—or death." He slapped his hand with his metal glove, bringing up a nasty red welt. *Pain. Pain will suck out my agony!*

"But, sir!" said Field Marshal Dono, his bent back and arms a parody of military stiffness. "The Overlord demanded immediate departure for the search. If he discovers you've dawdled, he'll have all our lives."

"The vat-shit bluffs, Field Marshal. He *needs* me now . . . else it would have been my spine and innards exposed to the crowd. No, Dono. The insult, the humiliation needs to be relieved, and that can only be done on the field of honor."

Dono thought about this for a moment. "Well, there is one of the captured human rebels who has been particularly troublesome. However, he is big and powerful."

"What!" spat Torx, grinding his teeth, his eyes firing up like coals. The metal studs in his black leather uniform flashed in the light as he strode to his underling and grabbed him by the front of his starched uniform khaki shirt. "Are you implying that a mere piece of muscular human scum can beat me, Torx, champion of the Continental Games!"

"Sir!" choked Dono. "With all respect, that was twenty years ago. You are a valiant fighter indeed, but neither of us is as young as we once were."

Torx released his grip, storming back to his desk and pounding a fist on it. "Damm it! I'm as good as I ever was, and I will *not* fight lessers! The best, Dono. I and my honor demand the best!"

"Very well, sir. I shall go and ready the prisoner."

"We shall fight above ground in the open air and the sun," said Torx gruffly. "Not down here in this fetid stinkhole."

"And what shall be the weapon, sir?" said Dono, recovering his professional aplomb.

A little twitch of a smile relieved the sternness of the BrainGeneral's face. "Chainsaws, Dono. I feel like getting a buzz."

The beginning of the end of human domination of the Earth was the development of the highest form of independent mutant mobile intelligence—IMMIs—and their deployment with the various mutant troops in battle and on call for battle.

These were later dubbed BrainGenerals, and the name stuck all the way through the Last World War.

BrainGenerals were simply a specially bred line of mutants, developed specifically for military command, and nothing else. When the human commanders of mutant troops rapidly discovered that they had an uncomfortably high attrition rate on the battlefield, a great many of them rapidly changed careers, leaving a wide-open gap in mutant leadership. One bright Princeton boy named Ralph Notkin had been studying the subject of intelligence in mutants for several years. It was he who suggested the development of BrainGenerals in the U.S. Military Task Force—America's kamikaze mutant troops—and the members of the Pentagon jumped at the idea. Within two years, America's mutant warriors gained a terrific edge in combat with the deployment of mutant leaders. These mutants were creatures of prodigious tactical and strategic skills, as well as absolute berserkers on the battlefield, engramically programmed with every martial art known to mankind. They had the genius of Genghis Khan and the spirit of John Wayne. Their real edge, however, was that, like the lesser warriors they commanded, they had absolutely no sense of self-worth. They were dedicated to carrying out the orders of their masters—human beings—with the utmost of the samurai spirit of honor.

For a few years.

Unbeknownst to their self-satisfied human masters, these BrainGenerals formed secret societies to practice a curious nihilistic neo-Buddhist religion, much modeled on Japanese secret societies based on codes of honor. When, as was inevitable, intelligence agents stole the secrets of engendering mutant intelligence, other BrainGenerals began to appear for different sides among the many warring factions of the world. Those governments had no way of knowing that the BrainGenerals of the United States made sure that their peculiar religion was communicated to the alien counterparts. Within ten years, every BrainGeneral had secretly and with evangelical zeal planted simplified versions of Zen Dementia (the human term for the religion—the BrainGenerals merely called it The Way) in their troops. Within twenty years, the dogs of war turned on their masters—and the masters, caught trusting too much their weapons of war—although they certainly fought back hard and long, suffering losses estimated up to two billion souls—found themselves slaves.

And thus the New Humans came into power, and mankind, whose scientists had created them, suddenly found themselves relegated to the status of "sub-human."

BrainGeneral Torx prided himself on the number of subhumans he had killed. His one regret was that he had been vatted too late to participate in the Great Mutiny.

This particular specimen of the breed before him, however, was a particularly magnificent species of subhuman, and for a moment BrainGeneral Torx almost regretted his decision to relieve his frustrations by meeting a subhuman on the field of honor.

"BrainGeneral Torx, I present to you Ronald Linton," said an underling, snapping his fingers. From a tent emerged several other bent underlings, holding a man in chains with a musculature and weight that almost made Torx blink with shock. The man must have been six feet five in height, with a chest the size of a bull's and biceps like hams. The man grinned at him through broken teeth with arrogant defiance that sent a chill through Torx even greater than he'd felt at the deboning of the chiropractor that morning.

However, he did not twitch or respond in any way. There was, after all, his stoic honor to maintain, and a BrainGeneral could not for a briefest of an inkling show fear.

He leaned over to Dono. "Heavens, Field Marshal. Is this the best you can find for me?" Making sure that this Linton fellow heard his voice.

The man just stared at him with icy blue eyes filled with hate.

"Ah, perhaps he is below your lofty capabilities, sir, but here is an added bonus in choosing this Linton fellow. Apparently, he was once a homosexual lover of Maximillian Turkel, for whom the vermin retains some affection!"

"Mother of God! What lies!" said Linton, fairly frothing at the mouth. "You fucking bastards." He almost tugged his guards off their feet as he lunged toward the mutants. "We're *friends!* Don't you assholes know what friendship is?"

"We know, scum, that male friendship among you subhumans generally entails a rear-entry position," said Dono. "Or did you merely suck each other's genitals?"

Cursing, the human captive lunged toward the Field Marshal. He was restrained by his chains, his large pectorals and biceps looking as though they were about to snap his bonds. "I'll kill you! I swear, I'll *kill* you!"

By the Holy Vat itself, thought Torx, cringing inside. What has my Field Marshal fool brought to me? I know what I said to him, but I thought surely the creature had *some* discretion!

"Pah!" said Dono, strutting before the captive like the martinet he was. "It is you that shall be killed by the great BrainGeneral Torx this day, on the field of honor! And I shall personally defecate on your remains!"

Don't taunt him, you idiot! thought Torx. But of course he could say nothing.

A little smile touched the suddenly still prisoner. "Field of honor, huh? What, is this gladiator stuff? I get a penknife and BrainBozo gets a howitzer?"

47

"No, of course not!" cried Dono. "Weapons will be equal. Of course you are far inferior to the BrainGeneral and must prepare to die."

Those huge muscles rolled and the man grinned. He didn't look as though he were resigning himself to death at all. Not his death, anyway. "Yeah? What weapons?"

Dono stood to his full four-feet-eleven-inch height, and a self-satisfied smirk split his face. "Chainsaws!"

The crowd who had gathered about gasped and clapped, getting more and more eager for the spectacle.

"No kidding!" said the man. "I used to be a lumberjack. Used to fuckin' *juggle* the things. Sounds like fun." He directed his smile toward the BrainGeneral. "Hey Brainy! What's the deal? I win, I get let loose?"

"If you win, subhuman," intoned BrainGeneral Torx gravely. "Then your eventual death, after your interrogation process is through, shall be swift and merciful instead of slow and tortuous. You have my word of honor."

"Gee, what motivation. Oh well. Let's get to it then. Let her rip."

"Soon my general shall *slice* that smile off your face!" said Dono tauntingly.

"Hey Brainy. I win, can I have a go at the dwarf?"

Torx said nothing. He simply stared at them both impassively for a moment, and then ordered the weapons brought forth. He had been mad to allow Dono to prepare this match for him, but now there was no turning back. Although he felt cold fear touch his spine, to show it now would be disastrous. No, he had to go through with this. Such was the Code of

The Way—and BrainGeneral Torx was nothing if not a devoted follower of his species' glorious religion.

Quickly, lumbering soldiers staked out the field with rope. This would be the Court of Battle. Then a number of Gun mutants surrounded the court, with orders to shoot the captive subhuman should he attempt to escape. Finally, a ceremonial wagon rolled out, driven by a uniformed man on a tractor. Bright feathers and flowers covered the top of this wagon.

Dono again, thought Torx. The whole ceremony was ludicrous, but the Field Marshal fairly skipped with happiness to the wagon and pushed open the lid. A tinny fanfare of trumpets sounded from speakers. "Your chainsaws, sir!"

"I got to fight with these bracelets on?" asked the man in chains.

"Release him!" said Torx. "And then give him his weapon." Torx then took off his cape and handed it to his attendant. He wore his metal-studded black leather uniform, and even as he stepped into the Court of Battle, he could feel his mind entering his combat meditation.

The chainsaws were streamlined and short, designed specifically for battle, not for cutting down trees. The prisoner admired his for a moment but then got a baffled look on his face. "No cord? How does this thing start?"

"The button on the bottom," called Dono. "Watch you don't turn it off in mid-battle—this happens to subhumans quite often!"

That *idiot!* thought Torx. What would the creature do next, tell him Torx's dueling weak points?

"Oh yeah? Thanks for the advice, shorty!" The man touched the bottom of the chainsaw, and instantly its motor whirred to life. "Wow, this sucker is fast,'' he said above the din. He wobbled it around a bit. ''Nice balance, too. I think this will be a pretty good fight, don't you, Brainy?''

Torx eyed Dono coldly, then pushed the button on his own machine. The motor whirred to life. The blade disappeared into a blur.

BrainGeneral Torx assumed the warrior's stance for the required two seconds, and then stepped toward his opponent. The crowd roared out its approval.

As he moved toward the man, even though it was a warm day, Torx felt as cold as the snow that still capped the Rockies in the distance. It was a bright, clear day, and the high-up sun glistened on the chrome of the rebel human's chainsaw. There was not the faintest trace of self-doubt on the man's face. It was more than mere defiance—it was like an embrace of death, if death was his lot.

Such humans were more dangerous than the fiercest of berserker mutants in the heat of battle.

Both men held their chainsaws in their left hands, and it was readily apparent to Torx that the prisoner was well acquainted with the strategies necessary for dueling with chainsaws. It was, unlike swordfighting, not a matter of parrying and striking. The chainsaw was secondary—one's skill with one's feet and free fist was paramount.

BrainGeneral Torx feinted and then, with a blood-curdling scream, ran to the left and then attacked with a fierce kick followed by a slash of the chainsaw.

The rebel not only dodged the kick easily and stepped aside blithely from the whirring blade; he swung his own weapon with a facility that almost chopped off Torx's hand. Only a last moment's twist saved him.

Torx stepped back and regrouped.

They fought.

Hacking, slashing, gouging, and attacking, they fought inconclusively for fifteen minutes. Torx realized that he was sweating like a pig under his leather. He was horrified to look down and see four separate slashes runneled with blood. Enough of this foolishness, he thought. Am I not a master of the martial arts?

He pressed the attack once more.

Unfortunately, the human was no novice himself, it seemed. He handled the chainsaw with the ease of a fencer with his rapier, and Torx soon found himself on the defensive. For a time, he thought he would lose the fight, and this would be his last day of life.

The man pressed in an attempt to prove Torx's suspicion correct.

A powerful blow of a fist connected with Torx's jaw, knocking him back and onto the ground.

With a scream of triumph, the rebel jumped toward his quarry, chainsaw flashing.

However, it was not to be Torx's day of death after all: the man stumbled on a hole dug up by a dipping chainsaw earlier. Torx was not only able to roll to the side, he was able to leap up and, with savage authority, slice through the exposed abdomen of the man with his chainsaw.

Blood splattered the roaring crowd.

The man went down, spasming, the grin still on his face.

"You lucked out, didn't you, bastard!" he said, and died before Torx could finish him off.

Torx bent over, heaving with his exertion. Such a fight he had never had before. Was he getting old? Growing soft? Surely not!

Field Marshal Dono capered over, dancing about

the fallen rebel. "To-ray, to-rah! Right again is the victor! The great champion has succeeded again! The magnificent BrainGeneral is supreme!"

No, thought Torx, standing, his chainsaw still whirring. It was Dono's fault that he had almost died today. All Dono's fault.

"Hail!" Torx cried. "I salute my fallen foe!"

With his cry, he executed the sweeping Brain-General salute with his chainsaw. Along the way, the chainsaw neatly sliced through Field Marshal Dono's neck.

The astonished head toppled to the ground. Spurting blood, the little body twitched, windmilled its arms, and then slammed to the ground.

The crowd grew silent with shocked horror.

Raising his eyebrows, BrainGeneral Torx examined the handiwork of his salute.

"Oh, dear," he pronounced. "A most grievous accident has occurred. I proclaim this day to be a day of mourning for our fallen comrade Field Marshal Dono. He shall be boiled and revatted with full military honors this evening. All hail, my dear and true companion in arms!"

BrainGeneral Torx turned off his chainsaw.

Too bad he wouldn't be able to attend Dono's funeral. He enjoyed funerals.

No. He had other matters with which to concern himself.

Turkel.

Maximillian Turkel had to be found, and soon . . .

It wasn't just a matter of the death threat from the Overlord. No, BrainGeneral Torx lived and breathed death every day.

No. It was a matter of honor.

Snapping his fingers for the assistance of some First Aid mutants, he went off to deal with his wounds.

Then, he thought, looking down at the bloody ruin of his outfit, he would have to see about a new uniform.

CHAPTER 5

"Hello, Jenny," whispered Jack Bender, sliding through the back door of the workroom.

The girl started, looked up from her work on the table. "Jack!" She smiled. Good. She was actually happy to see him. Most times Jenny was pleased when he showed up unexpectedly, but sometimes she was in a bad mood and didn't like getting spooked. "You're always popping up at the strangest times. Let me guess. You want to have lunch."

"Nah." He tiptoed over and kissed a perfect smooth pink cheek. Even though she wasn't wearing any perfume, Jenny Anderson smelled real good, like fresh hay and flowers, and he couldn't resist giving her a hug.

"You just can't stay away from me?" Jenny said hopefully.

Jack cringed a little inside. He'd been seeing Jenny for almost a year now without seeing any other female, and it was clear that the girl was hoping that this meant he wanted to volunteer to be her exclusive breeding partner. That is, get married, in the before-the-war vocabulary.

The muties allowed this, of course, only if it met their needs. If it was deigned that two slaves were biologically compatible and would produce genetically sound offspring, then monogamy was acceptable, providing that Biocontrol kept tabs on the reproduction aspect. However, the mutants were just as happy if humans acted like rabbits, mating where and when they pleased—just as long as they could analyze pregnant females and abort zygotes deemed unsuitable to the Cause. From time to time, there were forced matings, but with the strengthening lately of the human gene pool with the occasional switches of males from work farm to work factories or some other slave station to offset any possible inbreeding, this was not often necessary. Besides, the whole human reproduction was academic anyway. With their advanced biotechnology, if the mutants really wanted a certain combination of sperm and egg they could just take sperm and eggs from selected stock and gestate a fertilized ovum in the privacy of one of their vats. Naturally, however, mutant reproduction was of paramount importance in the vats; besides, any subhuman use irredeemably soiled both machinery and nutrient broth. "Clean" reproduction vats were vital to the mutants, because this was the only way they could reproduce. They were all sterile and had to use biotechnology to create more of their number.

That was one of the main reasons they kept human beings around. Try as they might, there was a dreadful phenomenon that occurred to fourth- and fifth-generation mutants without the addition of human genetic material in the mix: a genetic fading. Because even though mutant chromosomes and enzymes and DNA odds and ends could be adjusted, mutant reproduction was basically parthenogenic. Pure fresh human genetic material was needed to maintain older lines of mutants, but, most importantly, without it there was absolutely no hope of creating new, *superior* lines of mutants.

Although he was unfamiliar with all the technical terminology, Jack Bender knew all this. His friend Phil Potts knew a great deal about lots of scientific stuff, and had more or less acquainted him with the system. It all fitted with what Jack had observed in his life on the farm complex, so he accepted it readily enough, interpolating it all with the birds and the bees.

"That's true enough," Jack said, breaking the nuzzle. "Actually, though, today . . . well, Jen, today I need a *big* favor."

She blinked her pretty blue eyes. "And just how big is this favor, pray tell?"

"Well, you know how I've been stocking the hut?"

"Yes. And by the way, don't we have a date to head over there tonight?" An insouciant smile touched her lips, dimpling her mouth.

"Right. Uhm . . . yeah." He could disappoint her later; right now he needed the stuff. Jenny was on the staff of the complex's MedCenter. He could get from her what he needed to treat Max Turkel for the time being. It would have to hold him until he could get to a proper physician and get those bullets out. "I sure haven't forgotten. Really looking forward to it. But anyway, I thought, we should really stock the place with some serious emergency first aid supplies."

"Yes. Good idea."

"Can you, uh, like *borrow* some from here?"

She winked. "I think that won't be much of a problem."

"Bandages? Antiseptic? Cotton? Hypodermics and drugs for pain?"

56

"My goodness, you really want to cover all the bases, don't you? I'll get whatever I can, Jack. I'll bring it all tonight after dinner, okay?"

"Actually, I was kinda hoping you could get it for me now, Jen. The seeder's out for the day and I've been stocking and cleaning up the place and I've got just the spot to store it."

She looked surprised. "Wow. Now?"

"You know how I am. I get something in my mind, I want it right away. Instant gratification."

"Yes. I know what you mean." She looked over at the clock poised above her paperwork. "Yes, things are slow today and it's almost lunchtime. I can get you some stuff." Her eyes twinkled good-naturedly. "But you know, Jack, I'm a lot like you. I like instant gratification too, and there's maybe something I want now."

Jack shrugged. "All I can say, it's a damned good thing I'm young, the way you go on." He leaned over and gave her a wet kiss on the lips. "Supplies first though, huh?"

"Stay here and I'll be right back."

She'd gotten him gauze, bandages, ointments, hypos, and painkillers, and lots more he didn't even know the use for, and put them all in a large nondescript carry bag, the sort that the human workers used all the time and therefore would not be noticed by mutant guards, supervisors, or workers. Jenny was an efficient person, and Jack was showing her his appreciation exactly the way she wanted it. The bag full of supplies lay in the corner of the linen closet. Jack supposed that if Max Turkel had made it this far, he could make it an extra ten or fifteen minutes.

"You're sure your bosses won't miss you?" Jack said.

"What, on a nice day like today? Lunch hours we get to go outside and eat. And it is lunch hour, you know." She nibbled on his ear, and then sighed breathily as he buried his mouth clumsily into her neck, starting to unbutton her blouse with fingers already shaking and impatient with young desire.

"Oh, yes, Jack," she whispered, closing her eyes and arching her long and pretty neck. "Yes."

She wore only a kind of scarf arrangement as a bra, which was easy to untie. Jack had seen pictures of the support underwear that women used to wear back in the prewar days in some of Phil Potts's old books and magazines. He had absolutely no idea how guys got their dates out of them, and was happy for these simpler days. When Jenny's large breasts hung free, he proceeded to fondle, stroke, and kiss them. He had absolutely no idea what he was doing, but Jenny seemed to like it all just fine.

She was leaning against a shelf stocked with towels now, her head back against the soft linen, her young pert breasts outthrust like an offering.

Jack slipped his hands down her back and grabbed her firm buttocks, and she gasped with the muscularity and strength of the move. She thrust her groin against his, and sighed with gratification at its hardness and readiness.

"We haven't got much time, Jack. We'd better make this the—oh!—sporting sort."

Jack swallowed, his throat getting dry, his heart hammering like a wild beast in a cage. "Quick and dirty, huh?"

"Well—dirty, anyway, okay?"

It all would have been simpler if she was wearing

an old-time dress like in those ancient tattered magazines. But the mutants only issued pants, and so they had to fool with her belt and peel them off and everything. He could smell her excitement as she kicked the too-large trousers over her workboots; he could sense the wetness there in that thatch of dark pubic hair, stark against the milky-white hips.

He didn't have to take off *his* pants, fortunately. He just unbuttoned his fly and groped around in his underwear.

Meantime, Jenny stepped to a table and leaned over it, spreading her legs and smiling at him with an eager urgency.

"Okay, Jack. Okay, I'm ready."

"Yeah, I am too. Let me just get it out."

"Goodness, you'd think you had enough practice in the latrines!"

"The sucker's not swollen to four times its normal size when I use the latrine." He laughed, and she joined him. "Besides," he said, "it's worth the wait, huh?"

"We'll see."

"Oh yeah! You just wait!"

"I think that's exactly what I'm *doing*, Jack. Now hurry up before they come for the evening bed linen!"

Jeez, the girl certainly took the romance out of things. But it was enough to soften him enough that he could slip his penis out. He stepped over and rubbed himself against her and he got right back up to snuff. She seemed to inhale him with her pubis and before he knew it he was in instinct land and they were making like the famous Great Two-Backed Mutant.

Jenny huffed and chuffed and snarled and grabbed at his arms, her nails biting into them.

59

He just started pounding her harder.

She went out of control, her fingers slipping under his shirt and grabbing and scratching away like nobody's business, digging up some fresh epidermis among all the scar tissue there from previous Jenny-bouts. She was a moaner and a shaker, and so Jack was grateful for the muffling the linen must provide in the closet—one of the reasons this place was one of their trysting spots.

"Gosh—gosh," he was saying, getting out of control. When the rush of orgasm bloomed, it was particularly strong. "Fuuuccckkk!" he said, and collapsed on top of her, spent.

"Jack Bender!" she said, pushing him to get off her. "Whenever did you start using a foul word like that!"

Jack blinded. "Uh . . . well . . . Potts. Yeah. I been talking to Phil too much."

Jenny was already up putting her pants back on. "Well, you better not let the muties hear you say it!"

"And *you* better not let the muties hear you say *muties!*" A little disheveled and embarrassed, he rearranged himself as best he could. A good offense was generally the best defense. He sure as hell didn't want to tell her that it was his new friend Max Turkel out in the tree house now who had gotten him talking like this. Jenny was spunky enough, but she was no rebel, that was for certain. She was every bit as happy and complacent here as Jack Bender always claimed to be, and it would do him absolutely no good to let her know that he was hiding a major human lib leader back there, nursing him back to health.

"Okay. I was just a little shocked, that's all," she said, tucking her shirt back in. She went to him and kissed him softly on his cheek. "Thanks, Jack. That was just what the doctor ordered. I trust we still have that date tonight."

"Uhm . . . Oh, yeah, sure Jen." He'd have to figure out a way of steering her away from the tree house. But that didn't have to happen until later. Right now, he just had to get these supplies out to Max.

"Did you hear about the disappearance?" Jenny said as they went back to her work station.

"Oh, yeah. I guess they just figured out a way to get out of this place."

"Are you happy here, Jack?"

He had to act like he hadn't been thinking about the subject at all. "Sure! I don't want to go anywhere. Anyway, *you're* here, right?"

She smiled brightly. "Good. You know, all that stuff that Phil Potts talks about is all very good and maybe he's even right. God knows there are things that aren't wonderful about being . . . well, let's face it . . . a slave. But I guess if you accept it, and you live with people you care about and try to make the best of it . . . well, it's okay. You know? I mean, there are other things to being human than being free. And being free these days means getting hunted down and shot at."

"Took the words right from my mouth, sweetheart," said Jack. He hefted the bag onto his shoulder and waved her a cheerful goodbye. "See you later!"

He had more pressing things to worry about now than either Jenny Anderson or the relative merits of human slavery to human freedom.

He had a wounded man back in his tree house who needed attention and care.

CHAPTER 6

When Jack hoisted himself back into his tree house, the first thing he noticed was that Max wasn't there.

On the mattress where he had lain where bloodstains and the bottle of corn liquor. The bottle, Jack saw, was quite empty.

"Rats!" said Jack, tossing the bottle back down. Where could he have gone? Was he okay? What the *hell* was going on?

After some thought on the matter, Jack realized there was only one possibility. He'd seen no new bloodstains on the ground below. Turkel must have gone up.

He went to the set of stairs on the tree trunk leading to the roof, climbed them, opened the hatch, and peered out cautiously.

A smiling Max Turkel regarded him from a relaxed pose, leaning against the bark. "Hey, kid. Got the stuff?" His words were slurred and his eyelids were at half mast. The man was definitely the worse for drink.

"Max! What are you doing up *here?*" It was then that Jack noticed the pistol in his hand. It was Jack's gun, an old Colt .45 that Jack kept cleaned and oiled and up here, just in case. "And what are you doing with my gun?"

"Just wanted to make sure you came back alone. Just wanted to make sure I had a chance if you didn't—or went out fighting."

Jack was hurt. He couldn't hide the pout. "Gosh, Max. I wouldn't do that!"

"Hey, nothing personal, kid! I didn't think *you* would turn me in. I read people well enough. No, I just didn't know what was waiting for you back at the old corral, ya know?"

Jack immediately felt better. "Oh. You must be doing better, to get yourself up here."

Turkel shrugged. "I had some liquid inspiration."

"So I see. I got the stuff. You want me to patch you up down there or do you want to do it in the fresh air."

"Goddamn, it *is* awful fresh, ain't it? No, much too healthy. Let's do it below, if I can haul my ass back down there without it draggin' too much."

Jack helped him back down and settled him on his mattress.

"Like I said, we can't do much now. If you won't see a doctor, I'm going to have to get some of those books my friend Phil has."

"Just get me some more of that rotgut. Great stuff."

It looked as though it was going to be a bloody job, so before Jack got to it, he took off his shirt so it wouldn't get dirty. As he was pouring out water in a basin from a canteen, Turkel crowed from his matress. "Oooh wee! I see you took a few moments for wet refreshment yourself of a warmer nature back at the old homestead!"

"Huh?"

"Those scratch marks on your back . . . They look fresh and they look female."

Yikes! He'd forgotten about his back. Jack felt a warm blush start on his face. "Uhm . . . well uhm . . ."

"Hey, shit, don't be *embarrassed!*" Turkel chuckled weakly. "I'm just impressed, that's all. Hell, kid, the only thing I like better than killing mutants is romancing the ladies."

Jack returned to taking out the supplies, examining them, and placing them on his makeshift table for easy access when he got down to work. "That's a strange top-two list."

"Oh, I've got other weaknesses. Booze for one. And a good smoke. You wouldn't have any more tobacco, would you?"

"That stuff will kill you!"

"Sure, but a mutant will probably get me first. But you didn't answer my question."

Jack grinned. "A boy has gotta have his little rebellions. Sure. I got a little plot near the fields. Grow some tobacco, and some marijuana, too. Which one you want?"

"Christ, and I read you for Joe Clean-Fella. Just an old-fashioned surgeon-general's nightmare will do fine."

"I don't smoke the stuff much. Mostly I sell it."

"Ah. An entrepreneur as well."

Jack regarded him. "So you want the smoke before I get to work?"

"Sounds like a good idea."

Jack went to a drawer. He pulled out a box from which he extracted a hand-rolled cigarette. He offered it to Turkel and then used a homemade match to light it for him. The man sucked in a lungful of smoke appreciatively and let out a stream of it through his nostrils as Jack turned back to the materials on the table.

"So, what's her name?"

"Jenny."

"Cute?"

"I think so."

"Nice body?"

"What is this, an interrogation?"

"Christ, kid, I'm about to go under the knife. I want to think about naked babes while I twist in agony."

"I don't know, Max. Seems to me that you're doomed to survival, even though I suspect that you've used up most of your nine lives by now. And as for the agony . . ." He poured antiseptic into a rag and turned to face his rebel guest. "For right now, it's just going to sting a whole bunch."

And apparently it did, too, and more—but through it all, Max Turkel uttered not a word or a groan.

As Jack suspected, none of the bullets had hit anything vital. Two, in fact had exited—Turkel only had two lodged in him, one in his thigh, the other in the meaty part of his side. Both were accessible to tongs and a little digging, and so, with Turkel's permission, Jack went ahead and dug them out right then and there.

It wasn't like he'd never done this kind of thing before. He'd been trained to deal with animal husbandry and vetting, and so he wasn't squeamish about blood. There'd been the time a couple years ago when one of the bulls had escaped and the mutants had stupidly shot it. Not well enough to kill it though, and since it was prime breeding material, Brown 46 demanded that Jack get those bullets out and save the poor creature.

Jack had pulled it off too, somehow.

Compared to that, this was a song. Jack didn't even need Phil Potts's surgery books. Fortunately, Jenny had included a needle and stitching thread, and so Jack was able to pull the wounds together up tight, if a little raggedly. From all the other nasty scars on the man's body, he didn't think that Turkel would mind.

"Good thing I drank all that booze, kid," he said when Jack was pretty much finished.

"For the pain?"

"Yeah. Right."

Turkel closed his eyes and passed out.

At first Jack was upset. Had he hurt the man that much? But then he noticed Turkel's easy, rhythmic breaths. The guy was going to be okay, then, Jack knew. He sighed and allowed himself to relax.

Well, there was no way that Jenny was going to be able to come here tonight. But what excuse could he give her that she wouldn't get too suspicious too fast?

He looked down at the unconscious Max Turkel. "Okay, guy. So what am I going to do with you now?"

But Jack had a feeling—a very *definite* feeling—that something had changed in his life.

What it was, he wasn't quite sure.

Max Turkel healed.

He healed cantankerously, eager to get down and have a look at his crashed plane and frustrated when Jack refused to let him out of the tree house.

"You've got to stay still and rest for a while, huh? I don't want you popping stitches!"

Max agreed only if Jack kept him well supplied with booze and cigarettes. Jack did so reluctantly and simply because he figured the stuff would be the only thing to keep the man from climbing down the tree barehanded when Jack hid the rope ladder.

At any rate, after a few days of eating and drinking and talking, Max looked much better, and Jack thought that he'd be able to let him out of the tree hut for a walk or something. The rebel leader certainly was restless enough, and it didn't really pay to keep a big, robust guy like him cooped up too long. God alone knew what would bust loose when Max got down to the ground, but by that time Jack was more curious than afraid.

Max had talked to him. A lot.

He'd told him of the world beyond. He'd told him about the movement—the effort by thousands of other human beings to throw off the shackles of their bondage to the mutants. He told him of their dreams—and his dreams.

"Look, kid. We humans have got to face it. When we created these things, we really blew it. We're just damned lucky they need us, or they'd just kill us all off. Now, ideally, I'd like to do that to them . . . Though, I must say, they're not all bad, the muties. I mean, they are from human stock, so there are a few good ones running around. What I'm after though, really isn't total destruction of mutants. Hell, they're around to stay. And you know, I kind of suspect that a lot of humans maybe like it, being slaves. I guess lots of human beings have always been slaves, always will be. But thousands of us, man—we want that sweet taste of liberty again."

"But if there are mutants everywhere, how are you going to accomplish that?" asked Jack.

"What we need is our own country."

"Oh, right. The mutants are really going to let you have one. The only piece of land they want you to have is six feet under."

"Too true. Actually, we haven't really decided what piece of land we're after. We just want to fuck things up for the muties right now, spread the word, get new members."

"Right. And you think you're going to sign *me* up? Forget it!"

"Hey, I don't see a pen anywhere! Look, Jack, I owe you. You be your own slavish person if you want to be. But since I happen to have your ear right now, you want to listen to a guy that's got some fucking *experience* in this sorry excuse for a world? You probably haven't even been off this complex, have you?"

Jack shut up. He had to admit that Turkel was right. He hadn't been off the complex—as far as he knew. In his youth, there was the possibility that the muties had taken him off to a larger installation for testing or whatever the hell they did to young boys. But if they had, he'd been unconscious and he didn't remember anything. No, the only experience of the rest of the world he had was through Pottsie's old books and pictures.

Which was just fine, thank you. Jack Bender knew exactly where his ass was safe and where it wasn't and how far he could tilt it from one zone into the other. And that was the way he liked it.

Still, it didn't hurt to listen, he guessed. He happened to have some time on his hands . . .

"Yeah, okay, Max. I guess maybe I *should* hear your story."

"Well, gosh, farmboy. Thank you very, very much for the privilege." Turkel winked at Jack, instantly relaxing the tension that had been building between them. "Actually, you're just like I used to be, Jack."

Jack blinked. "You were raised on a farm complex?"

"You bet your balls I was. Why do you think I give you such hell. 'Cause you stir up the old memories in me! Christ, I would have sold my soul to the devil himself to get away from seeding and tilling and harvesting." A big fat grin split his dark, hairy face. "And come to think of it, maybe I did just that, now, didn't I?"

"If you did, it was the devil that got the shitty deal!"

Turkel roared with laughter and clapped Jack on the back. "That's the spirit, Jack Bender! That's the spunk!"

He then settled back to tell his tale.

Maximillian Turkel grew up on a mutant farm complex in Salinas, California—an area as famous for its agriculture as the Midwest bread basket. He had lived, he said, a life much like Jack Bender's. Not a bad life. Plenty to eat, plenty of sex, plenty of recreation. But there was something missing . . .

"You see, the mistake the muties made, Jack, was putting me in Salinas."

"What's so special about Salinas?"

"Well, it's about nine miles from Monterey Bay, maybe fifteen to the ocean, and on clear days with the wind coming strong from the west, you could *smell* it, and there would be these seagulls . . . Now, much like your friend Potts, there were those who had pictures of stuff outside, stuff like the sea. But you know, you couldn't *smell* those pictures, and what was coming in—well, Christ, it was incredible. I must have had some bastard sailor's blood in me, 'cause it would always drive me nuts. Finally, when I was in my teens, I finally got the nerve to ask my mutant superintendent if maybe I couldn't get a field trip out to take a look at the ocean. Just for a little while . . . just maybe to splash around in it. Well, this creep— and as you are probably aware, they never made creeps before like *mutie* creeps—he just sort of stares at me like I'm a Martian who's come down to tell him that his fly is open.

" 'Of course not, you little snot. How dare you suggest such a thing.' And I get put into detention for three rest days running. Well, my personality started changing toward its perfectly pissed present form, let me tell you! Fuck you, asshole! I thought while I was doing my detention hog swabbing or whatever. You're going to be sorry for this—and I'm going to see the ocean!

"So it took me three years to figure out how I was going to do it, and inside that time, I learned from smuggled literature that there were rebels within the system and outside the system. And I think to my- self—I want to get *outside* the system. Now, like you, we had our leashes. A periphery too. Cross the line, the beeper goes off . . . And the bastard mutie who was our supervisor claimed that maybe there was even an explosive device that would take your head right off if you crossed that line . . ."

Jack self-consciously touched the hard little node in his neck which was just such a device.

"But I made friends with the underground at the complex, and they told me that there was a way to fix that. A surgical method. So when I figured the time

70

was right, they cut open my throat and pulled that bastard out and sewed me back up . . . not much better than you did, come to think of it. I had a rucksack, a contraband gun, and some ammunition . . . and a map. I knew where my contact would be. My career in the underground outside was already started before I even got out . . .

"But I had to take care of one more thing before I headed toward the sea."

He cleared this throat dramatically. "You got a compost maker here, kid?"

"Sure. Shreds up leaves and wood and crap. Why?"

"Let me give you a little piece of advice. It does a pretty good job on mutie supervisors, too."

Jack cringed at the thought—but nonetheless got a vicarious thrill at the thought of old Brownie getting tossed to the blades. Bastard was probably so tough he'd break 'em, though. Still, it was a sweet idea.

But of course not Jack Bender's cup of tea.

"That's all very well and bloodthirsty, Max. I've never told you this before—but I decided a couple years ago, I'm a pacifist. So you might as well forget about instilling all that revolution crap in *my* breast."

Turkel grunted. "Yeah. Sure kid." And went on with his story.

Apparently, Turkel's career in the revolutionary movement—at least the one on the continent of North America—had been filled with highs and lows. The problem, according to Max Turkel, anyway, was that until lately the movement was not united, but rather a bunch of factions that tended to fight among each other as much as they fought the mutant oppressors. The inside underground, of necessity for survival, had to be much more cohesive. The outside underground, loosely and occasionally linked with the inside, could not have existed at all without the halfsies.

Jack was, of course, familiar with the halfsies. He'd seen them in the complex's town center, on trading missions. Occasionally, at harvest time, the complex would hire a bunch to help with a heavy workload. Essentially, halfsies were a mix of mutants and humans who made up at least half the population of the world—people who were not part of either the military-industrial complexes of the world, or of its agroproduction complex. They were the fodder populations, the dross, the people who made up the rest. The mutants would probably have just killed them all off but for the fact that they served a purpose—and as they grew in number, they were no real threat and soon became too unwieldy to exterminate. It was among the halfsies that mutants deemed unsuitable were banished if they were not outright fed back to the vats. And it was among the halfsies that genetically inferior humans lived. Occasionally spot checks were made and aberrantly brilliant and talented humans were found and extracted. The actual truth was, Pottsie said, that the mutants needed this larger human pool as much as it needed the gene pools in its complexes. Genetics were predictable only up to a certain point—true genius and startling qualities tended to be flukes as often as not, and the muties needed that fluke factor. Anyway, the halfsies served their economic purposes and had other values as well.

And, of course, they allowed excellent cover for Human Liberation Front underground activity.

It was in this milieu that Turkel worked for years as a guerrilla soldier, hitting mutant supply lines, complexes, military bases, and whatnot, all in the effort of diminishing mutie power. However, as a mere foot soldier in the offensive, he often found the attacks either frustratingly futile or downright stupid. The muties paid little attention to the guerrillas' silly efforts, content to lose the occasional soldier if it meant they could just ignore the rebels, like a giant ignores gnats gnawing on its earlobe.

"So what I did," Turkel explained, "I learned not just to be a good soldier, I learned to *lead!* And I learned to organize. Didn't take long for me to start up my own intelligence methodology, and I began to figure out just what the muties were up to and where a few lobbed grenades would do the most good."

"Just what *are* the muties up to, Max?" said Jack lightly.

"What, the North American muties . . . or muties in general?"

"Both."

An ominous darkness filled Turkel's eyes and they became, for an instant, unfocused. "No good, Jack. No good at all."

"Hey, what kind of answer is that?"

Turkel recovered. "Shit, kid. Don't dig too deep if all you want to be is a tractor boy on Toadstool Farm."

Jack shrugged. "Fair enough." Nonetheless, the comment—but more particularly, the haunted look on Turkel's face—bothered Jack for a long time to come.

Turkel continued his tale. Soon, he had become the equivalent of a general of the liberation forces. He'd been through a lot—twice he'd been caught by mutant forces and had managed to escape before they killed him.

"I've got a reputation with 'em now," he said, grinning that treacherous smile. "Kind of a stinky

Robin Hood. Problem is that they've got a reward out for me among the halfsies . . . And halfsies are often as not just as rotten and corrupt as the lower mutants. Nice thing, though, among the halfsies, you can disguise yourself pretty easy.

"Anyways, to sum things up, there's a base up near Canada. If I can get my sorry carcass there, I'll be all right. And I'd like to do it some time within the next decade or so."

"You really think you can fix that plane?"

"I sure would like to. I don't see making it very far on foot, not unless you're hooked up with some kind of underground railway for rebel leaders."

Jack shook his head.

"Nope. Didn't think so. Well, you say you got some material I can use? Some tools?"

"Yeah. But you gotta rest, Jack."

"Fuck rest. I'll rest when I die. I gotta get *out* of here!"

"Okay, I'll make a deal with you. You stay flat on your back for one more day. Day after tomorrow, I'll have the stuff for you . . . And if I can get away long enough, I'll even help you. I'd like to learn about planes, anyway."

"Okay, we'll learn together. Just kiddin' . . . I picked up my share of info about them."

"I'm an excellent mechanic, and I'm a better learner."

"And you're awfully modest, too! Say, weren't you supposed to have a little tete-a-titty with that Jenny broad tonight?"

"Yeah, but I told her I had an emergency here."

Turkel's eyes grew wide. "You didn't tell her about me, did you?"

"No. I told her I dumped chemicals and stuff all

over the place here and it smelled like hell and I had to save a bunch of stuff.''

"Smart kid.''

"So, you know, you say you know about guns and martial arts and like that. Maybe you can tell me some more.''

"I thought you were a pacificist.''

"Hey, yeah. But I'm not *stupid!*''

Turkel laughed. "You just aren't honest with yourself. You're as bloodthirsty as the next all-American blooded kid.''

"Americans?''

"Yeah. Once upon a time, there was this country . . .'' Turkel's eyes got distant again. "A country where liberty was king. You know, I never told you . . . When I busted loose from my farm complex . . . I went out to see the ocean, kid. I don't suppose you've seen the Pacific Ocean have you?''

"No,'' said Jack, his eyes growing huge with curiosity. "What's it like, Max?''

"Christ, it's God's own swimming pool! Blue as a pretty girl's eye . . . Breezy and with foam on the waves . . . And the smell . . . Jeez, kid. It smelled like what life is supposed to be. I still go to the ocean when I can. Too bad you won't go with me sometime, Jack. But no, Jack Bender likes it just fine on the his farm complex.''

Jack shrugged and turned way. "You never know. The muties are getting looser. Maybe they'll start taking us on field trips someday.''

"Yeah, right. And maybe the bulls will start giving milk!'' He sipped at his cup of corn liquor. "Yep, Jack Bender. With your help, I'll be out of this place within two weeks tops, and up there at the North Dakota base. I got people waiting for me up there. And we've got some serious plans to cause some serious trouble for that bastard Overlord Charlemagne!'' Another sip. ''Yep. Good ole Smitty. Good ole Jenks. They'll know I'm not dead. They'll be waiting for me with a cigar and a cold beer!''

CHAPTER 7

"Maximillian Turkel!" snarled BrainGeneral Torx. "Where is Maximillian Turkel?"

Fredrick "Smitty" Smith spat out a tooth mixed up with an unhealthy amount of blood. "Who?" he said weakly.

Torx smacked him again, hard, the chainmail gauntlet leaving harsh marks against the man's wrinkled, weathered skin. Smitty groaned, but said nothing more, held fast in the grip of two huge and muscular armored mutants with snouts like pigs.

"You stupid rebels. You think we won't get the information we want from you," said Torx coldly, pacing, the metal heels of his boots clicking on the wood like Thor's footseps echoing from Valhalla. "It just so happens that for amusement as much as for their usefulness, I brought along a couple of specialists in crucifixion. It looks like this was a wise decision on my part."

"Okay," sighed Smitty, all but spent. They had him outside the headquarters while the buildings burned orange and red, a chill spring breeze from the lake guttering them like wicks amid melted candles. The air smelled of death and tasted of singed blood and promised doom. But the eyes in Smitty's beaten face remained sparked with defiance, staring at the mutant BrainGeneral with hatred. "Okay, you know he's not here, right? You wiped us out. You got us—isn't that enough?"

"You think we care about his little annoyance of a rat's nest?" The BrainGeneral's fungus-blemished face twisted with contempt as he stared at what was left of the complex which had been nestled, camouflaged. "No. We want Turkel. Where is he?"

"Look, I swear! You know as much as I do! I thought he got wiped out with the rest in the Kansas air base raid."

"He escaped in a single-propeller plane." Torx gripped the man's chain in his mailed glove with a strength that threatened to crush it like a man might crush an eggshell. "He was headed *here*, subhuman! Here!"

"That's fucking news to me, pal! Believe me."

The BrainGeneral ground his large powerful teeth together. The sound was like a sanding machine attacking unglazed ceramic. "I cannot afford to believe you, subhuman Smith!" His eyes glittered with desperate anger. "Detachment Five!" he harshed, his voice ice-cold and monotone, reverberating as though he had a megaphone embedded in his larynx. "Front and center! We have a subject for your talents."

Smith said nothing, just stared down at his feet, as though steeling himself for what would come next.

Detachment Five consisted of three Class J mutants, their large, muscular arms drooping from hunchbacked shoulders as though they'd been extracted from gorilla DNA rather than human. Class J were mutants specifically manufactured expressly for the indelicate art of forced interrogation. This particular species, the Point Threes—the Crucimutants to the rebels—were heavily built specifically to lug around large wooden crosses from place to place—the traditional mode, after all, for proper crucifixion. This muscularity, as well as their pinning abilities, made them particular favorites as right offensive guards for mutant football teams.

The Crucimutants, however, carried no cross with them now. They were among trees, and trees would do just as well. Their wide, contorted features leered, sprouting fangs that arose willy-nilly from purple lips like a wild tooth garden. A particular grotesque arrangement of polyplike growths dangled from their long chins and neck, like shredded dewlaps. They wheezed with expectation as they grabbed their intended victim and looked to their leader for direction.

"That big oak over there should do."

"Lateral or horizontal, BrainGeneral, sir."

"Whatever is the slowest."

They nodded, wheezing as they carried Smith toward the wide oak.

Suddenly a scream so loud that it even stopped the Crucimutants cold washed across the scene. It wailed for a full moment, and then died out with a ululation of hopelessness.

"Ah. That would be one of your daughters being raped by a few Class P boys," stated Torx as mildly as though he were just announcing that it was time for lunch. "Did you know that those fellows have barbs on their penises? Hell on military-issue underwear."

"Stop it!" cried Smith. "Don't hurt them. No more! I swear I don't know where Turkel is. Please, stop it!"

"Specialists, I do not remember telling you to halt," said Torx. "Continue your duty."

"No! No! Oh, Jesus . . . *Jesus!*"

79

"Oh yes, one of your gods, true? An appropriate cry."

The rangy mutants hurtled the man against the bark, his feet dangling a full yard from the ground. They pulled up his arms and then, with lightning speed, air-hammered thick iron spikes through his wrists with special guns attached to their arms like metallic growths. They repeated this quick procedure on his ankles and then stepped back, their purple-mottled faces splashed with their victim's blood.

Smith hung from the tree like a gasping fish from four hooks, his eyes nearly popping from his skull.

"It's simple," said Torx. "Tell me where your leader is, *give him to me* . . . And you will be spared. As well as whoever remains of your mate brood." The last term dropped from Torx's mouth with utter distaste. "Well, subhuman Smith. I assure you, that is not the only trick my dogs know. Shall I set them on you again?"

"I . . . don't . . . know."

Torx nodded to his Class J henchmen. "Proceed. I think this is a stubborn one, but transcribe everything and present it to me later."

The Crucimutants were, like many mutants, equipped with numerous skin-flap pockets, similar to those in marsupials only not for gestation purposes, but to carry tools and equipment. Metal and wire clinked as they pulled instruments of torture from these—instruments especially designed for drilling work on nerves already under stress from crucifixion. Normally, BrainGeneral Torx would have lingered to watch. However, since this did not look promising (Perhaps the man was telling the truth and he indeed knew nothing of Turkel's whereabouts? Oh well, too bad.) Torx moved on. There were other, more important matters to attend to.

Torx strode amid the devastation as coolly and remotely as some mobile statue. There was no compassion in his heart for the dying and the dead humans strewn over the ground like fallen bowling pins. He did not even rejoice at his victory. He was entirely focused upon his goal: the successful capture of Max Turkel.

Maximillian Turkel! Maximillian Turkel! The name pounded in his head like a never-ending refrain from a bad song.

Maximillian Turkel!

Such was his preoccupation that he did not notice that, from the wreckage of building, a human toddler was crawling directly into his path. It was a little boy less than one year old and he was dressed in an ancient set of PJs with faded clowns against pink. He crawled out, blind with the tears runneling down his face, searching for his mother. It was only a sudden wail that brought the BrainGeneral up short.

He halted, and he looked down.

The little thing was wailing below him with a voice much bigger than his small form.

For some reason, the baby looked very much like Maximillian Turkel. But then, all the subhumans looked the same.

Annoyance filled BrainGeneral Torx. He lifted his heavy metallic boot and with a swift, decisive move, he brought the cleated heel down on the baby's face.

The skull, as it was crushed, made a satisfying squishing and popping sound.

Torx strode on, a tiny glow of satisfaction lighting him from within.

That felt good.

Outside the burning and the destruction stood one of the Bloodhound squadron half-track vehicles with which the troops had stormed the place. In the back of a vehicle, leaning against the tailgate and looking as though he was about to be ill, was a human. Guarding him were two Bloodhounds—dog-faced mutants with enormous snouts and ears whose hearing and sense of smell were acute.

Torx stopped and regarded the man.

"Jenkins," he said, wiping his bloodied boot on a clump of grass.

"BrainGeneral Torx," whispered the man with a tone of fear and respect.

"He is not here, Jenkins."

"I told you, dammit. I told you that! You've blown me, Torx. You've blown my cover."

Torx shrugged. "There will be other subhuman rebel rat's nests. Other covers."

"It took me *years* . . ."

"And thanks to you, though, we knew where to look. Which was why we spared your life."

"If you had waited, I could have give you Turkel. If he's alive, he'll come here."

"We can't wait that long."

"No. You're not a patient . . . general, are you?"

"Have you any idea of where he could be?"

Jenkins shuddered. "Just draw a line on the map between the Kansas base and here. He'll be along that line somewhere."

Torx nodded. "Of course."

"What about me?"

"What about you."

"What are you going to do with me—now that this is over? If the survivors see me alive, they'll know I'm a traitor."

"We will ship you back to Denver where you will be reassigned, Jenkins . . . after a thorough debriefing, of course. You shall undergo plastic surgery and a slight scrambling of personality and mannerisms. Then, as I intimated before, you shall be planted among the halfsies where you can infiltrate a den of rebels, just as you have done here."

Jenkins looked up and out over the destruction and death that had consumed the place like a wing of black and flame.

A shrieking cry rose up among the burning and the groans.

Jenkins looked away. "You must really want that poor bastard Turkel."

"I think, subhuman," said BrainGeneral Torx. "That 'want' is much too mild a term!"

Grinding his teeth, he looked up and out past the smoke and the rubble.

Somewhere . . .

Torx could *feel* it.

The subhuman was out there, somewhere . . .

CHAPTER 8

"Jack!"

The man started, looking up from the bench where he was working. He recognized the voice, and he flinched inside at the sound of it.

"Jack Bender! *There* you are! I've been looking all over for you!"

Jack turned around, dreading the confrontation. He'd been putting it off for as long as he could, but still he knew he'd have to face it . . .

She was standing there at the other side of the workbench, hands on the hips of her fresh jumpsuit. Her long blond hair was brushed nicely, and she looked as fresh and healthy as spring flower—and about as eager to pollinate.

"Oh, hi, Jenny."

He stuck some tools and glue and stuff into the large bag, already bulging. Wouldn't do to let Jenny have a look at exactly what he had in there, though. Might give her some clue as to what he and Turkel were up to—the refitting and rebuilding of a light plane. No, that wouldn't do at all.

"What are you packing?"

"Shhh. Tools to work on the tree hut with. I'm smuggling them out there and I'm *not* going to be able to keep them there too long."

"Jack, what about *me?*"

"You need to get worked on too, Jen?"

She shook her head disgustedly. "Yeah, in a manner of speaking."

"I guess I have been kind of neglecting you lately. Sorry, it's just that once I get involved in a project—"

She stamped her foot, a pout appearing like a storm cloud on her face. "It's some other woman, isn't it?"

Jack had been lifting up the canvas sack. The remark caught him so off guard that he let go. It crashed back down onto the bench with a dissonant jingle. "Huh?"

"You've been taking some other female up there, haven't you? You've got some young teenager or something . . . I always thought you looked a bit too long at that set of fifteen-year-old quadruplets in the dairy. Manure! Between them, with those wobbly mammaries, they make up a whole cow themselves!"

"Jen!" said Jack, truly dumbfounded. He walked to her and tried to put his arms around her. "Jenny, sweetheart! You know that for me, it's only you!"

She pushed him away. "Come off it! You're a guy!"

"I may look, Jen . . . But here . . ." He touched his heart. "Here, I only think about you!"

"So how come you haven't been taking me up to the hut and *showing* me you care!"

"I told you. I've been working on it . . . And then that chemical spill . . ."

"That was *days* ago, Jack. Surely it's aired out by now!"

"Yeah, I guess so . . . But I still got work . . ."

She turned to him, suddenly silky and huggable again, a smile underlying the seductiveness of the pressing, soft curves of her against his chest and abdomen. "Oh, take the night off. I've got weaving and pottery class tomorrow and the next night and I won't be able to see you then."

Cripes, thought Jack. Not with Max there. "Uhm . . . Jen . . . I don't know."

She pressed a knowing hand against his groin. "I'll make it well worth your while, Jack." A clever little tongue described the length of her red, moist lips. Instinctively, he reached for her, but she danced back and away, her eyes sparkling with mischief. "Not unless you let me come up to the hut tonight, Jack!"

"Okay. Okay. But give me till eight o'clock, huh? At least that way I'll have the mattress clear."

Of Max Turkel anyway, he thought.

"Okay, lover. Eight o'clock. With bells on my nipples." She kissed him quickly on the lips and then ran away.

"Ding-a-ling-a-ling," said Jack Bender, turning back to his bag of tools.

As though he didn't feel in a fix enough, Jack Bender was walking out of the mechanics shed when he almost ran into Brown 46, his mutie supervisor.

Fortunately, Jack saw Brown before Brown saw him. Jack moved back behind the edge of the building, dropping his sack as quietly as he could. Brown had been out there, talking to another mutant. Some guy that Jack had never noticed on the farm before.

Jack peered around the corner to see what was going on—and whether he should start planning on some other travel route.

Brown was handing some kind of envelope to the other mutant. Jack could only see him from the back, but from the looks of him, he was a Class A mutie— a breed not developed for their fighting prowess but for planning and strategy backups for the Brain-

Generals. Some As also worked in scientific studies. They were slender with stooped shoulders and a strong neck to support a big head, bulbous with brains. Jack had seen their kind here before, advising supervisors on grain storage or genetic planning or weather control or what-have-you. This guy, though, with his nose that looked like a truncated carrot and stringy hair like stewed kale—he'd never seen this one before, and for some reason, the warped little creature gave him the willies.

"You sure you told her to meet us here?" he said in a raspy little voice.

"Yes!" said Brown, blustery and reddening a bit. "She's usually very punctual. I don't understand what could be the matter."

"The information is all here in the packet?"

"Yes! Of course. I'm a Chosen—not a subhuman!" said Brown, rearing to his full self-righteous height.

"She is a good spawner, then?"

"Yes. Fertile. Very fertile."

The thick, lopsided head nodded. "Very good. The planning in these matters is important. Your cooperation in this project is appreciated, Brown the Fourth, Point Six."

"Excellent. Your appreciation will be illustrated in the usual manner, I trust."

"Naturally."

"Ah. I see her now. She is but two minutes late. We must forgive the subhumans—they have absolutely no idea of the importance of punctuality."

Jack saw a girl approaching. He recognized her as Hazel Larkin, an eighteen-year-old he'd been flirting with seriously in his visits to the dairy section. No actual contact, though; that was exactly the time that Jenny had arrowed into his life. He dived back behind the corner; if she'd looked, Hazel would have seen him, and he didn't want that, not yet. But he was curious; just what was going on here, anyway?

"Ah, Easel, I am happy . . ."

"Hazel, Master Brown." Demurely and sweetly and obediently.

"Yes, of course. Hazel, this is Knox the Third, Point Five. He's a doctor with Reproduction Section of the Midwest Quadrant. I just wanted to show him a member of our proudest stock."

"Thank you."

"You are a strapping youngster, child," wheezed Dr. Knox. "I am pleased that you have reached the age of reproduction . . . I am only sorry that the rules demand maturation to the age of eighteen . . . I'm sure you could well have borne several fine offspring by now worthy of the Cause."

"Thank you, Master Knox."

A moment of silence. Brown's irritated voice broke it. "Well, don't just stand there looking pleased with yourself, child. Open your blouse!"

"Yes, sir."

Knox placed a scabrous hand on Hazel's left breast. "Yes. Yes, very nice indeed. Plump and good consistency. You shall suckle many young, I'm sure, Hazel. You may button up now and leave."

A feeling of nausea and disgust, mixed with anger, struck Jack deep down in his gut. Damn them! he thought. Damn them to— He caught himself up short. No, he was thinking too much like Turkel. He had to take all this objectively. You had to be *objective* in this existence, in order to survive.

And, above all, Jack Bender was a survivor.

So instead of running out and strangling the bastards for molesting his fellow human being, Jack bit back hard on his anger and stayed put.

"Come," said Brown. "There is another I wish to show you."

"Of course."

Jack could hear their voices disappearing in the distance. When he figured they were gone, he hoisted the sack of tools back onto his shoulder and ventured out again, almost running into Hazel.

"Jack! Well howdy-do to you!"

"Uhm . . . oh, hello, Hazel. How's the, er, dairy business?"

"Churning and cheesy, as usual." She was a striking brunette with faintly almond-shaped brown eyes and a mole on her cheek. An image of Hazel, when she was just post-pubescent, skinny dipping in Rocks Lake arose unbidden in Jack's mind; she had moles on other parts of her body as well. A faint odor of sour milk wafted about her. For some reason, Jack found it curiously exciting.

"Oh, great. Bye."

"Hey, wait. You still solitary with that Jenny girl?"

"Uhm."

"Oh, too bad. I wouldn't mind having a baby with you, Jack. We'd have some fun making it, wouldn't we? Anytime you want to have some preliminary practice, just let me know, okay?"

Jack shook his head. "Ah . . . thanks, Hazel. Thanks a lot."

She winked at him and then waggled away.

Jack, for a moment, could not take his eyes off the sway of her hips. God help him, what was sex *doing* to him?

Whatever it was, he rather liked it.

Hoisting the sack up, he headed back toward the twilight and his hut in the trees.

Things really weren't so bad, Jack thought as he entered the woods.

He was in good shape with Brown; as he'd promised, he'd gotten his section well seeded, and the area superintendent had given Brown the credit. He was well into his next set of agricultural duties, and so he could afford to take time off.

Jack had learned very quickly that since the muties regarded human beings as basically inefficient, almost fools, when it came to duties, it was not wise to prove them too wrong. If you operated just above the bare minimum expected, you were lauded and received rewards. Jack found that by really putting the pedal to the metal when he needed to, but not letting the muties know just how *quickly* he could do things, he earned himself *lots* of spare time. This gave him the needed edge in keeping up his lifestyle; which is to say, he could futz around in his tree house or with some mechanical gizmo, he could dally with a woman (just Jenny now, of course) or just go fishin'—figuratively or, if he had a mind to—since he was pretty wicked with a bloodworm or a fly—literally.

Of course, all this took some serious dancing around his mutant-assigned activities and watches. But, until lately, this particular Iowa complex had been nothing if not calm, and the mutants did not work hard to make sure their slaves were exactly where they were supposed to be.

And, curiously enough, considering the disappearances lately, security had not tightened at all.

Jack Bender of course had no time to be anything but grateful for this, and was just happy now that he'd gotten out of the main complex's work buildings (the actual town was several miles away) so he could head out to his haven.

He had to get Max out of the tree house.

It was unfortunate, but he was going to have to take Max Turkel at his word and let him out to hide somewhere else while he dealt with Jenny's need for amorous attention. It wasn't that he didn't trust Jenny. He knew she'd be as concerned about Max as he, and help in any way she could. No, it was just that this stuff was *much* too dangerous and he didn't want to get her involved. Perhaps there was just a tad of worry also that once she met the virile and adventurous Max Turkel, she might throw Jack over and run off with the admitted rake—but mostly, he just didn't want any possibility that she'd get hurt in any way.

He'd rather die than have that.

Jack dug out the climbing spurs and proceeded to scale the tree to the hut. When he hauled himself in, he immediately smelled the by-now familiar fumes of recycled corn liquor. But now, it seemed particularly pronounced.

In a moment, he knew what had happened.

Damn his eyes! The bastard had found the extra bottle that Jack had secreted in one of his bottom drawers.

Sure enough, there he was, stretched out and snoring like a Sleep mutie doing overtime research, two pint bottles by his fingers, both empty.

"Max!"

No response.

"Max," he said, kneeling down beside him. "You know, I really don't think this stuff is going to heal you."

No response.

Jack shook him.

Max grunted. "Take 'im out, Slug. Nail the fucking bastard!" Then he flopped back onto the mattress.

"Max!" Frustrated, Jack went over to one of his canteens. No way was he going to be able to get Max Turkel down the rope ladder in this condition! He'd fall and break his silly drunken neck. He opened the canteen and dumped a quick four ounces on his passed-out guest.

Max spluttered awake, immediately reaching out and grabbing Jack's throat. "You're not going to take me! I swear it, you're not going to take me alive!"

"Hey, cool it, Max. It's just me! Jack!"

Max blinked the water out of his eyes, saw Jack, and immediately let go. "Wha— What happened?"

"You've been drinking too much, Max."

"Christ, whaddaya expect? I'm so bored here, nothing to do but drink!"

"Okay, you've got your wish then."

"Huh?" It was surprising to see Max Turkel at a loss for words.

"You can go. In fact, you're going to *have* to. Somehow, you're going to have to climb down the rope ladder without falling on your face, and then you're going to have to go hide in the bushes awhile."

"Jeez. Why?"

"It's Jenny. My girlfriend. She's suspicious. She demanded to come here tonight, so I said she could. She'll be here in about a half hour."

Max smiled lasciviously. "Gonna lay some pipe, huh, kid?"

"None of your business, Max. Now, you gonna sober up or do you think you can get down the rope drunk?"

"Shit, I once blasted five muties to kingdom come, squiffed out of my mind on home-brewed beer!"

"Good for you. Then a few rungs will be a song to you."

"Sure, kid. Whatever you say. You've been real good to me. Now, I don't suppose you brought along another bottle of that fine corn to keep me company on this cold evening, did you?"

Jack shook his head. "No. I'll give you a blanket. Now get up. I'll put the ladder down and—"

"Jack!"

Another voice. From below, on the ground.

"Oh fuck," said Jack Bender. "It's Jenny!"

"Hey kid," said Max, weaving drunkenly. "Can I get sloppy seconds?"

CHAPTER 9

One of Hazel Larkin's favorite things to do of an evening was to go out and walk along Rocks Lake and watch the sun set and the stars turn on in the sky.

She didn't have to have company, although when she was younger she'd bring a girlfriend and these days, as often as not, she had along a boyfriend to spoon with as the moon silvered the lake and the crickets started to chirp. Now, for example, she was alone. She felt like being alone now; she had some thinking to do and some contemplation. Not about that creepy mutant who had pawed her just a little while ago. That had happened before and it would probably happen again. It was part and parcel of being a slave who was meant to breed. The muties, being sterile, had an ambivalent fascination about fecund subhumans. The way mutie women looked, actually, Hazel didn't blame the mutie males for copping a feel from time to time. She wondered vaguely if they could even get erections.

She certainly hoped not.

No, she needed time to think about the changing time that was upon her—the time in which she was expected to start bearing babies. She definitely didn't feel ready for the task, although she didn't mind the stuff you did with guys to obtain those biological results. She was, though, like most women, more than a little intimidated about the enormity of what she faced. She was not a particularly introspective girl, but she wasn't dumb and thoughtless either, like some of the females in the dairy who talked nothing but prattle and silliness.

No, birthing babies was a *responsibility*.

And a body—and God knew, a mind—had to give responsibility proper thought.

It was a mild enough evening, although the darkness did promise a bit of a nip. Hazel Larkin was glad she'd brought a sweater. Now as she walked along the lake, the breeze gently rocking the leaves that hung from branches into the water, she was surprised to find her mind wandering away from the subject of sex and pregnancy and babies into other subjects—or simply into a gentle lulling peace.

That's what Rocks Lake gave to her. Some peace of mind. When she was alone, anyway. She'd told this to Phil Potts, and he'd called what she did alone "meditation"—which Hazel Larkin supposed was right. You didn't feel good, you gave yourself a spoonful of medicine—meditation. That's what she was doing now.

Rocks Lake really wasn't natural, and it really wasn't a lake; it was too small for that. Actually, it was more like a pond, Phil Potts said. A lake was much bigger, and though it could be man (or rather, in this case, mutant) made, it could be natural too.

Phil Potts certainly knew a lot, thought Hazel. He sure was smart. Maybe *he* should be the father of her first baby.

She had to admit, though, she'd much prefer the preliminaries to be with Jack Bender. Of course, if *that* happened, Jenny would scratch her eyes out and then bury her in the cesspool. No, she couldn't have a baby if she were dead.

Only part of Rocks Lake was bordered by trees; the rest was plain grass lake, except of course for Rocks Creek that fed it and Rocks Dam that stopped the creek up. It was the wooden area that Hazel favored. She particularly liked to sit on the craggy rocks there, throw pebbles into the water, and watch the ripples through the reflections of the moon and the stars as the sweet smell of blooming trees and the smell of the water calmed her.

She sat down on a rock, picked up some pebbles, and proceeded to do just that.

Splash! Plop! went the rocks.

She stood up thinking to skip a flat rock she'd found across the still surface of the lake. Just last week, Pete Martin had skipped a rock six whole times. Hazel wanted to see if she could beat his record.

Just as she cocked her arm back, though, she thought she heard something that shouldn't be.

A rustling in the large clump of bushes that ran between the trees just about ten yards away.

Hazel stared hard, but she couldn't see anything or anyone. Or hear anything more, for that matter.

She shrugged and put her attention back to skipping that rock. It was flat enough, that was for sure . . . The trick was to throw it at just the right angle so that the flat part would hit the surface of the water just so and then bounce off so that the process would be repeated a number of times.

Trouble was, girls weren't quite *built* in the way guys were. Their arms threw funny . . .

She tried a number of positions, but none seemed right.

If she could just get the right *angle* . . .

There! That was it!

She pulled her arm back to throw . . .

And a hand caught around her wrist. She started to cry out with shock, and another hand reached around her, holding a cloth that smelled strong and strange . . .

Before she had time for even another thought, Hazel Larkin collapsed into unconsciousness.

CHAPTER 10

Jack threw the rope ladder down to Jenny, and she struggled up. He pulled her up that last yard or so, and the first thing she did after she got to her feet was make a quick examination of the place, her nostrils high and taking their own inventory.

"Whew! You're right, Jack. Smells really *bad,* whatever it was you spilled. Kind of like turpentine mixed with body odor."

"Uh, yeah, right, Jen," Jack said, trying to hide his extreme uneasiness. "Maybe we'd better go somewhere else, huh?"

She smiled at him and put her arms around his neck, melting into him. "I can live with it."

"Well, maybe I can't."

"Try. I've been thinking about that mangy old mattress for days. There's absolutely nothing like it. When we get bonded, we're going to have to store it somewhere safe so that if we want to we can bring it out and use it for old times' sake."

"Gee, Jen, you know, it's such a nice evening out . . ."

She looked around, an odd expression on her face. "That's strange."

"What's strange?"

"You said you were moving stuff around, fixing things?"

"Yeah, I did, didn't I?"

"It looks pretty much the same to me . . . except all those sacks and stuff over there. Can I look and see if—"

He pulled her back and, having no other alternative, he took her in his arms and kissed her passionately. It was just the distraction she needed. She returned the kiss wetly and vigorously, and then pulled him down toward the mattress.

Excitement shining in her eyes, she began tugging on his belt.

He was going to suggest that a nice soft pad of grass outside might be much better, but her insistence and enthusiasm charged his own lust, already built up by stress and the memory of Hazel Larkin's proposition.

"I think I can do that myself," he said, and undid his jeans.

"Good, I won't be but a moment." Quickly she shed her clothing and even as he was about to take off his shirt, she was spread out before him, ready and waiting and already panting. "Jack, that's good, that's fine. Just do it. Do it now. I can't wait!"

He was feeling pretty urgent now himself. He fell atop her, made a few peremptory pawings at her breasts, kissed her neck once or twice, and then, his penis already about as ready as it ever got, charged in.

It was a really good thing, he thought right in the middle of the pounding and pawing, the snorts and the yelps, that this hut was miles from any mutant ears, because they sure were making a ruckus here now. The tree hut was actually shaking!

When it was over, Jenny turned over on her side and just drowsed off, a smile on her face.

Jack, however, was wide awake in a post-ejaculatory fog.

"Psst!"

Jack blinked. What was that?

"Psst! Jack!" A whisper.

Immediately, Jack knew who it was. Turkel! Who had *promised* to be quiet.

Panicking, Jack turned over and saw that Jenny was sound asleep. Thank God for that, anyway. Quickly, he got up, slipped on his trousers, and hobbled over to shut the drunken hero and rebel *up!*

Max Turkel was on the roof.

There had been simply nowhere else to put him, and it had been quite a chore to get the soused fellow up the rungs and through the trapdoor. And now that the rigors and preoccupations of lust had more or less quit Jack Bender, a realization stole over him.

Max had been up there the whole time, listening to him and Jenny make love!

Quickly, Jack hauled himself up the makeshift ladder and through the trapdoor, almost colliding with Turkel in the process.

"Jack . . ."

"Shhh! Would you be quiet! She's asleep, but you might wake her up. I told you to stay put!"

Jack shut the trapdoor behind him, taking a great breath of fresh air. It was dark out here, and he could only vaguely make out Max's hulking form in the dimness.

"Jeez, didn't I tell you? Besides a world class hero and cocksman I'm also somewhat of a voyeur."

Jack could feel himself blushing furiously. Only the humor and self-mockery implicit in Max's voice kept

100

Jack from punching him out. "Oh, wonderful. My good friend!"

"Sorry. Couldn't really help it though. I figured staring down through the trapdoor and hanging on was a lot safer. This thing was shaking like a son-of-a-bitch! Hell of a way to die, getting tossed off a tree house while Tom Sawyer fucks Becky Thatcher."

"Huh?"

"I guess there are a few books you've got to read, pal. Hell, I'm just maybe envious. That's quite a gal you've got there."

"Thanks. I guess."

"Like her, huh?"

"Oh yeah."

"Well then, she deserves the best then, huh."

"You bet. What are you getting at?"

Jack felt his shoulder being patted affectionately, solicitously. "Young man, I must say, you *are* an enthusiastic lover. Absolutely nothing wrong with you, I'll tell you that. Boy, if I had your stamina when I was your age, I'd have stayed on the farm and fucked my life away too."

"Yeah. So what?"

"The old vigorous in-and-out is just fine, but a woman like that . . . Shit, any woman . . . Well, they need a little finesse once in a while."

"Huh? You're telling me how to have . . . Sheesh, man. What are you talking about?"

"Whoa, there, don't kick me off the roof. I'm just trying to help! I've got about a quarter century of experience on you, Jack. I tell you, most men are so fucked up with competitiveness and macho bullshit, they don't talk about what makes a woman happy. Me, I've got plenty of both, but I've also got a big mouth and I'm a fucking busybody. So you wanna hear what I have to say, or should I just shut my fat trap?''

Jack had gotten past his outrage at Turkel's peeping tom antics and, he had to face it, his own hurt pride. The gears of his thinking machinery began to clank to work and he realized, there might be something *to* this.

"Okay," he said, a little sullenly. "Jenny's asleep. I'm listening, but keep it low, okay?''

"Sure, kid. It's like this." Turkel began to speak in low, confidential tones.

Jack listened . . .

And listened, nodding, fascinated.

And listened some more, until he suddenly balked.

"Euuk . . . You've got to be kidding me. That's where—''

"Listen to me, once you've had a taste or two, it's the sweetest-tasting thing in this world, pal. And besides, when is it that what you're eating talks back to you? And likes it in the bargain?''

Jack shuddered, a little doubtful.

"Come on, buck up, Jack. And take my word for it—it's fun. Now, the last word of advice is that you've got to follow not so much your instincts in the nitty-gritty business of amore, but rather your gut feeling. Let your feelings for her just dance out in your fingers, your mouth, your tongue . . . Play some music on that divine body . . . And shit, pardon me, I'm getting a little bit horny myself. Maybe I can actually just show you myself . . .''

Max started for the ladder, but Jack stopped him.

"No way, guy.''

"So you think you're man enough for it?''

Jack squared his shoulders. "You bet. But I swear

102

to God, if I look up and see your ugly face *watching*—I'll shoot it off!''

"Sure, kid, sure. You're going to thank me, I promise you.''

Jack went back down the ladder, making sure that the door was securely shut behind him.

Jenny looked up at him sleepily from the tousled sheets on the mattress. "Jack, am I hallucinating, or did you just come down from off the roof?''

"Right, yeah. Got a little, uh, science project up there.''

"Anybody ever tell you you're a *weird* guy?''

He put his hand on her side, just touching it slightly, the way Max had instructed. He let it slide down slowly, very gradually down the arch, letting it drift down her abdomen, across her belly button, and then down to her pubic thatch—but only lightly touching the ends of the hairs. Then he pulled the hand away.

He looked up at his girlfriend and she was staring at him as though she had just seen God Himself. "Jack! Wow . . . That was . . . That was . . . nice!''

"Yeah?''

"Oooh! Do that again!''

Jack shrugged. "Okay.''

He played with her back. He licked the back of her neck. He fondled her breasts gently, licking the nipples as worshipfully as Turkel had suggested. All as slowly, deliberately, and intelligently as he could muster.

Jenny took it all with a kind of stunned but enthusiastic awe. Gradually, this gave way to sighs as gentle as cornsilk and to low groans, all of which Jack found himself enjoying immensely.

He was hard as a rock, and normally this meant that it was time to start humping. However, as Max had ordered, he restrained his atavistic impulses. Instead, he slowly licked his way down her stomach to her pelvis, where he was confronted by what Pottsie called "The delta of Venus." Whatever it was, it was dark and aromatic and mysterious as hell.

Jack was suddenly stymied.

Just how exactly did you *do* this next thing, anyway?

He lifted his head.

"Oh, Jack. Jack, that's so nice. Love me, Jack. Take me." Her eyes were half lidded and dreamy, lost.

"Just a second, Jen. Musta drunk too much ice tea at dinner. Gotta take a whiz off the roof. Okay?"

"Okay. Okay, but come back *just as soon as you can*!"

"Oh, don't worry, honey. I will."

He found it difficult climbing with an erection, but the problem corrected itself by the time he crawled out on the roof, careful to close the door after him.

"Max," he whispered.

"Sounds like it's going great down there, kid. Why'd you stop?"

"Max . . . I . . . I, well, *I'm not quite sure how . . .*"

Max took this thoughtfully and seriously. "Well, kid, visualize this rich, juicy fruit with the core cut out, and this stem on top—"

He would have told her to keep quiet, to stop *screaming* and carrying on, she'd attract the muties, if his mouth wasn't full and busy, and he wasn't hanging on to her for dear life.

Actually, he was enjoying himself too much to say anything. Anyway, they were far enough out in the

104

woods. The muties wouldn't hear anything. And if they did, they'd think it was just a rabbit caught in a trap or something.

Jenny was bucking and thumping like she was attached to a live wire or something. Her arms were flailing and she was gasping something fierce. Finally, with one last spasm, she arched up into him and collapsed, breathing with astonished relief.

"Jack," said Jenny. "Jack. You never did that before . . . That was *wonderful*. Where . . ."

"Books. Pottsie's books. Sure glad he taught me to read. Looks like it's turned out okay, huh?"

She just grabbed ahold of him and hugged him for all she was worth. "What can I do for you?"

"Just a minute. I think nature calls again."

After he got back from off the roof, and sheepishly made his suggestion, her eyes got a little wide, but she smiled and nodded agreement.

And, surprise of surprises, she didn't need any instruction from Max Turkel, either.

Without qualms, she told him to lay down on his back on the mattress. Then, taking her cue from him in her slowness and patience, she stroked him until he was pointing straight at the ceiling even though every muscle in his body was super-relaxed.

When she finally took him in her mouth it was like wet velvet, only alive and unpredictable.

It felt as though she was pulling the very marrow from his toe bones, and when he came it was the absolute best ever, an explosion of urgent delight.

She snuggled up to him when it was over. "You know, I think we *are* made for each other."

"I guess so," he said, feeling as stunned as she was.

"I really should take a look at this book Phil Potts has."

"Well, I don't know. You seem to do just fine without it."

"Really?"

"Didn't I look like I was having a good time?"

She giggled. "You were so cute. I thought you were going to faint."

"Yeah? And what about you? I thought you were going to bang a hole through the floor."

"It felt like I did and fell straight through it to the ground and then went to *heaven!* Oh, Jack! I want to have your *babies!*"

"What does reproduction have to do with sex . . . I mean . . . uhm." They just looked at each other and started laughing uproariously.

A slow, delicious time later, just holding each other, Jack suggested that maybe it was time for her to go. He had to take care of something here and then he'd head back for his own barracks. Jenny reluctantly agreed, pouting only a little that Jack wasn't going to walk her back home. She left only after he promised that after her two nights of classes, she could come back and do this stuff again . . . and again . . . and again.

Jack had no problem agreeing.

When she was gone, the trapdoor in the roof opened and Max peered down. "I take it I can get off this goddamned roof."

"Sure, Max. Sure."

"Yep," said Turkel, lowering himself, clearly a great deal more sober. "I didn't listen, I didn't hear a thing."

Jack smiled. "What, are you deaf or something?"

"Well, I guess I did catch a groan and a gasp here

and there. But I didn't look, I swear I didn't look, though I was tempted." He was about to collapse on the mattress, then looked down and thought better of it, settling on a chair instead. "I just got one question."

"Shoot."

"Does that sweetheart have a sister? Preferably a *twin* sister."

"Eat your heart out, Max."

"It was gone long before you started moaning, kid. I don't know, Jack. Maybe I already shot my wad. Maybe two thousand satisfied women is my limit. Maybe this old love root is tired and worn out anyway." He looked down at his crotch, considering. "Nah."

They both laughed.

CHAPTER 11

When Hazel awoke, the first thing that she was aware of was that she was cold.

She opened her eyes.

Gosh, she wasn't only cold. She was freezing. Her teeth were chattering and her knees were knocking and it just plain felt bad, like maybe Heather Norton had left the window open in their barracks and a chill January wind was flowing through like an invisible river of ice.

It was only when she actually focused her eyes that Hazel Larkin realized that she was buck naked.

She was lying on some sort of bed with a waxy sheet on top of it, and she immediately tried to get off that bed, only she couldn't because her wrists and her ankles were tied by some kind of rope, fastened in turn to the corners of the bed.

No, *table*. It looked much more like a *table*, actually—the kind that Dr. Winston used, when she had her checkups.

Although Dr. Winston's office was never, *ever* this cold.

It was then that Hazel remembered the hands surrounding her, the smelly cloth in her face, and she felt a delayed reaction of fear, compounded by the even greater terror of being tied down. She was aware, then, that the medicinal smell lingered, along with other, more prominent smells. Chemicals, soap, and astringents . . .

And the strong, familiar slaughterhouse odor of old blood mingled with fresh.

The table was in the middle of a large room, walled by shelves containing equipment of such byzantine nature that their functions were far beyond Hazel's limited grasp. They were like a garden of Dr. Winston's and the farm's dentist Dr. Evans's surgical instruments, grown monstrous and grotesque, as though they themselves had mutated. On shelves just a few feet away, which she could see only if she twisted her neck, were huge bell jars of colored liquid, in which things floated.

Human hands.

Human feet.

Human heads.

It was then that the scream, which had seemed frozen and stuck in her throat, emerged.

The world went red and crazy for a moment. And then, when she was out of breath and could scream no more and was vaguely aware that she had screamed a very long time indeed, she heard the whirring, like a faint echoing of that scream.

It came to her, supported by a coiled stalk: a machine.

A machine with *eyes*.

They were huge, gaping eyes, glaring out from lenses, bloodshot, with black pinprick pupils. They seemed to have no lids—they just stared, eternally open, ravaging her with their intent stare.

"Ah!" a voice buzzed from a speaker grille on the machine. "You are awake. And in good voice. Noted."

Hazel blinked for a moment at the alien monstrosity. It was like nothing she had ever experienced before, so strange that it was far beyond nightmare. Nonetheless, she'd always been a spunky kid, and she was surprised to hear herself asking a question.

"Who *are* you! Why am I here?"

"It is *I* who will do the interrogation, subhuman female!" shrilled the voice, the grille buzzing with intensity. "Be silent and be not insolent, or you will suffer far more pain than otherwise."

Even as the machine finished speaking, more and smaller machines, all on their separate coil stalks, arose around her like tentacles of a mutant octopus. Each held a separate device. Hazel could see forceps and razor-sharp scalpels and hypodermic needlelike devices among less-familiar, even more frightening spined and barbed instruments. All displayed clearly to show the means of her increased pain.

"Don't hurt me," she said, feigning meekness that she did not feel. What she felt was a mixture of fear, outrage, and an intense will to survive.

"Excellent. Begging shows a contriteness much needed for the operations to proceed with alacrity." The tentacles crept up against the table, clattering against the metal but progressing no further, as though eager to sink their blades and saws and needles into the softness of her bare flesh, and yet somehow restrained. "Now then, female. What is your name?"

"Hazel . . . Hazel Larkin. Hey, you know, I'm colder than a well pump in February. Can I have something to put on?"

The eyes just stared at her for a moment. But then suddenly a machine on wheels hummed up to her, offering her a folded gray cloth.

"Hey! How can I put this on tied down?"

Tabs on the ropes restraining her unsnapped. She was able to sit up. She took the garment offered to her. The cloth proved to be a hospital shift. She quickly put it on. It was flimsy and it only came down to her thighs, but she did not complain. It was better than nothing.

"How old are you?"

"I was eighteen last March fifth."

"Do you have brothers and sisters?"

"I don't know."

"Do you know your parents?"

"No. I was raised in the communal family."

"Are you a virgin?"

"Yes."

"Then why is your hymen broken?"

"Hymen?"

"You are not a virgin, Hazel Larkin. Why do you lie?"

"All right. I've been with a couple of guys. So what?"

She had been noticing now that as she spoke, a large window was moving behind her. Well, not a window really, but something like it—it had some lines—squiggly and ragged lines that moved as she spoke. A graph, measuring something.

"Anyway, how do you know that?" she continued.

"You have been given a thorough examination."

"What do you want— Hey, I know. This happens sometimes, doesn't it? Just a kind of mutant spot check, right? Test us out. I get to go back to the farm now, right?"

The eyes just glared at her.

And then the questions continued.

They were silly questions. She had to answer puzzles and do sums and when she got tired of it, those

111

dreadful metallic guards moved in with their gleaming threat, and she rapidly answered the questions as best she could. It was grueling and it was long.

But then—suddenly, the eyes disappeared. The instruments shuddered—and then were still. The lights dipped to black, and then came back on.

"Brief power outtage," a nasal mechanical voice said. "Emergency power employed. Emergency power employed."

The instruments still weren't moving, though, and the eyes weren't back.

And her legs and arms were now free of the ropes.

It was time to walk.

She hopped off the table. The linoleum was cold on her feet, but she hardly noticed, so urgent was her need *to get out of there!*

She ran past tables filled with test tubes and laboratory gear. She ran past tables stacked with equipment that looked as though it had had been built for milking mutated cows. She ran past bubbling tanks filled with dreadful hunks and pieces of human beings.

She knew that if she stopped for a moment, an instant, then the terror would envelop her and she would be paralyzed and unable to move, let alone escape.

Escape. The word drove her on, relentlessly. She reached the wall. The door . . . Where was the door?

She ran along the wall, finally finding what she was looking for. It was an ordinary door with a knob, and her fears that it was locked gave way as the knob turned beneath her hand.

She opened the door and was about to run through when she realized that a squat figure was standing in her way.

112

"Going somewhere, Hazel Larkin?"

It was the mutant called Knox—the one that had examined her before with Supervisor Brown. The one whose head looked like a pile of flesh-colored cow-flop.

She shrieked and turned to run away.

The shaft caught her directly in the right breast, knifing through her chest and out her back. A coiled barb buried itself deep in her shoulder. Pain and surprise shot through her like electricity. More of the tentacle-thing surrounded her, lifting her up from the floor, bleeding like a side of fresh-cut beef.

And just before consciousness spilled away from her, those monstrous lensed eyes confronted her again as she wiggled on the hooks and the spear like a fish.

"Very well," said the tinny voice. "The flesh and the gray matter need not necessarily be *alive*."

CHAPTER 12

Ten days passed.

They were the densest days that Jack Bender had ever experienced.

On one hand, he had to do his farm chores, but he did those quickly and efficiently in the morning so that he could spend his afternoons with Max Turkel.

Max was much better, healing rapidly.

And he was also rebuilding his plane.

As fascinated with machines as Jack Bender was, he had never been so absorbed in a piece of equipment as he was with that plane. He'd always enjoyed reading the books that Phil Potts gave him about planes and aviation, and would always stop to watch the very rare plane that passed by overhead. However, this plane was the first he'd ever seen up close, and the process of repairing it and refurbishing its engine made Jack absolutely awestruck with wonder.

With this flimsy structure of light wood and wire, strapped onto a streamlined engine and propeller, a man could soar and wing through the sky like a bird.

A man could *fly*.

And suddenly, more than anything else, Jack Bender wanted to learn how to operate the thing. He wanted to fly, too.

Jack didn't admit this to Max. He was afraid that

admitting this fascination would give the edge that Turkel needed to talk him full of revolution nonsense. He could almost hear him in his dreams: "Well that's right fine, I guess, but how the hell are you going to fly inside the complex? No, kid. You gotta be *free* to fly. And good a time as you seem to be having here, growing food for the muties, providing fresh DNA, licking their asses and about to provide stud service to boot—well, sorry, but you ain't free. Now, on the other hand, if you let me dig that little radio thing out of your neck, we can just hop aboard this plane here and be off for wonderful and exciting places. See the world, kid. Join the Human Liberation Army—and Air Force, come to think of it!"

No, he didn't need that.

Still, it was very difficult to hide his enthusiasm and interest as together they slowly rebuilt the plane.

In general, the engine was in pretty good shape. Fixing this was where Jack's specialty lay. There was a piston shaft that needed replacing, and the distributor caps were about shot. It needed an oil change bad too, and a bullet had nicked the fuel line—not enough to lose any gas, or Turkel would never have gotten this far. Jack could improvise on all these pretty well just by cannibalizing some of the spare machines back in the mechanics shop. He wasn't surprised at the sorry maintenance shown by the muties. For some reason, the mutie engineers were really shoddy about simple things like changing air filters and oil and what have you. Maybe they thought that some specialized mutant existed, created solely for that task. As far as Jack knew, they didn't.

"You know, Max, I never did ask you. Why'd you choose to land in a forest?"

"Christ, kid. It was a clearing in a forest. And I

didn't have much choice. I was almost out of gas, and I felt like I was about to pass out. I saw the complex buildings in the distance and I figured that I had a shot of making contact with sympathetic, intelligent human beings. Unfortunately, I got you, Jack.''

"Cute, Max. Real cute.''

The stuff that was really fascinating and new for Jack was putting the plane's other parts back together—and, of course, the cabins, its controls . . . and especially what those controls did.

Fortunately, the propeller was in good shape. Jack didn't have the faintest idea of how he could get another one of those, and he sure couldn't repair it. However, the part called the fuselage needed some heavy body work, the flaps and ailerons were fucked, and the horizontal stabilizers were a mess.

"Well, the rudder looks okay,'' Turkel had said, scratching his head. "Thank God I can put one of these babies together in my sleep. Course I'm going to need your help with some of that carpentry stuff and body work you say you know. I guess I should just be happy that the engine's workable and the controls aren't busted.''

"Uhm—maybe you can tell me what does what.''

"Sure. Let's get this stuff out in the open and started up. When we've cobbled it back together, I'll show you how she runs. And maybe, just maybe, I'll take you out of this hole, kid.'' A wink.

Jack said nothing. He just threw in with his share of the work, listening and learning, adding his own knowledge where it was appropriate.

All in all, the pair got along extraordinarily well.

Max Turkel seemed to be just as pleased as punch in his role as pedagogue, teaching the young electroplowboy about the world. When they were too tired to work on the plane anymore for fear of making a mistake, Max would take him off into an area padded with grass and showed him some crucial elements of martial arts. And when it seemed as though only their mouths would move, Max certainly moved his, telling Jack exotic tales of weaponry, mad mutant armies, and just how warped and bizarre this world was.

"You know, a buddy of mine—gone now, and I promised him to bring down a case of cold grog to hell when I go—he said that the more things change, the more things stay the same . . . And that was what happened to Earth. It changed . . . But it also stayed the same. There used to be human nations, human governments, human dictators, human genocide; now there are mutant nations, mutant dictators, mutant genocide. Prejudice, starvation, disease, wars? We've got 'em, they had 'em. A rotten filthy stinking life and then you die—unless you're rich or high up on the social scale. Hey! The status quo continues. The only good thing back then, the only good thing now, is freedom . . ."

"Freedom, freedom, freedom. You sound like a broken record."

"Hey, don't knock it until you've tried it. Like I was saying, *freedom*. And I'll say it again. I've got twenty-five years on you, bub, and I can still whip your ass."

"Cripes, you're kinda touchy, aren't you?"

"I am when you disparage individuality and freedom, Jack. Anyway, where was I? Oh yeah. My friend says, yep, things aren't really the same—what they are is a *distorted* version of what things used to be like."

117

"What's that supposed to mean? I don't know what things were like back then."

"What about your pal's books?"

"They're just books and pictures—that's not like living it."

"Can't you say the same about freedom, Jack?"

Jack said nothing. He just turned back to his body and structural work on the fuselage.

Heated exchanges between Jack and Turkel were rare. Generally, they worked well together, and the closest thing they got to a tiff was when their friendly banter turned a little edgy.

What with his farm chores, dodging mutant scrutiny, helping Turkel with his plane, and getting instruction about the wide world on the side, to say nothing of the occasional necessity of bringing Jenny out to the shack and repeating their newfound love tricks, Jack Bender barely got any sleep.

Nonetheless, he loved it. He thrived. Within the ten days that it took to get the plane back into serviceable order, he had learned everything he could learn about how it was built, how it worked, what rudder or flap did what and to which stick and gear it was attached, to say nothing, thanks to the two books he borrowed from Pottsie, of the niceties of taking off, landing, and that wonderful stuff in between—flying.

Of course it was all in theory. None of it was practical; he had zero air time so far, though he hungered for it as a male virgin hungered for females, knowing the technique and theory of sex, and yet never having the actual *feel* of it.

In his dreams, though, Jack Bender flew.

He flew with command and authority. He flew with ease over mountain and river, field and ocean, doing loop-de-loops and power stalls, Immelman rolls (after which he shot a mutie fighter out of the sky) and dives to beat the band. In his dreams, he was the king of the air. In his dreams, he was free.

Once he awoke and there were tears of joy in his eyes. He just wiped them away, turned over in his barracks bed, ignored the snores of the other farm-boys, and went back to sleep until his predawn rising.

Jack, of course, noticed all this happening to him. What he did not notice was how influenced he was by Max Turkel in very basic and fundamental ways.

Jack Bender had never known his father.

Jack Bender had never known any of his brothers.

Max Turkel was rapidly filling in these deep and empty spaces in him.

Jack had been raised in the farm complex community by surrogate mothers who had cared for him, and taught by stern teachers, some human, some mutant—all distant and uncaring.

So it was natural that Jack would take to Turkel in this way—especially since Max Turkel took an equal shine to him.

Most importantly, Jack absorbed a vast amount of not only knowledge but vicarious experience in a very short time.

And though he did not realize it, it made him grow.

Jenny commented to him about this late in those ten days, after a particularly gentle experience of lovemaking. "Jack—you've changed somehow."

"Hmm?"

"You're different."

"What . . . am I *mutating* or something?"

"No. No, you just seem—I don't know, a little *older* maybe."

119

"Time passes, we get older. What you mean is, I've matured."

She held herself close to him, her sweet breath tickling his earlobe. "Maybe."

"Let me get this straight. I'm older, but I haven't matured that much."

She giggled. "Maybe you're just a pain in the ass."

"Is that what you're doing when we make love . . . groaning from the torture?"

She hit him playfully. "Silly. Of course not." She started playing with Jack's sparse chest hair, which she always made fun of. That was one of the many things that he envied about Max Turkel. The man had a veritable *forest* of hair on his upper body, sprouting out of the top of his shirt even. Jack had suggested that Max's hirsuteness was proof positive that man descended from apes. Max's only response was to ask for a banana and a mate in his next lunchbox. "I like the way you make love, Jack. I don't know *why* I groan. Would that be what Phil Potts would call a philosophical question?"

Jack had to laugh. "You bet. Maybe you'd better ask him. Maybe he'll know some profound truth on the subject."

"My goodness, you're getting flip. What's the word? Sarcastic. That's it. What's got into you, anyway?"

Jack had to bite his tongue. He almost blamed it on his new pal, Max Turkel.

"Anyway . . ." Tug of chest hair. "Speaking of making love . . . why don't we do it just one more time . . ."

"Jenny, it's not more than a half hour till midnight! Curfew time, remember?"

"One of those old-time quickies?"

"Jen, I'm about to drop I'm so tired." He certainly was—he'd been at work since before dawn.

"Well, then," she said persistently. "Drop on me!"

"Look, you know, there's a possibility I won't even be able to get it up!"

"That'll be a first!" she said, her hand sliding down to his crotch.

She quickly proved him wrong.

He made it back to the barracks with about thirty seconds to spare, the last ounce of energy in his body literally siphoned out.

Those were a very rich, deep, and intense ten days, so full of life and experience that Jack Bender had no time to think about what it all meant. Vaguely, at the back of his mind, he realized that, when they were finished with the plane, Max Turkel would simply get in and take off and Jack would never see him again.

He didn't dwell on this, though. His mind was so consumed with all the other things that he had to do, he had no time to think about how much he would miss the coarse, hairy, boisterous fellow.

And then, at the end of ten days, late one afternoon Max Turkel looked up from his work on the wing gear and said, "You know, I think this calls for a celebration tonight, Jack."

"Why?"

"It's finished. Granted it could use a paint job, but she's flyworthy now. Tomorrow morning we'll just haul her out to that strip you pointed out so cleverly. I'll take off and be out of your hair and you can spend more time balling your girl, huh?"

Nudge nudge. Wink wink.

"Uh, yeah, sure, Max. Great."

But Jack wasn't thinking about sex.

He was wondering why he had this strange lump in his throat.

CHAPTER 13

The human brain plopped onto the bare tabletop, red and gray and wet, quivering like a mound of frozen gelatin.

Knox the Third, Point Five leaned over, his gnarled finger pointing down at the veined gray matter. "The secret, my Lord Exemplary Torx of our Sacred Religion, lies in here."

BrainGeneral Torx stared down, nonplussed, at the gory remnant of a living being, and grunted. "Don't you think you should be a little more careful with the specimen, then, if it's so important?"

The mutant scientist shrugged, a chuckle bubbling from his bulbous lips, his own half-contained overstuffed brains wobbling about in their translucent sac. "I unfroze it just to show you the process, my Lord. As for being careful . . . Well, we actually only need a small specimen, a sliver if you will of the tissue for the genetic purposes that it will serve."

BrainGeneral Torx squinted, troubled and trying to think about what bothered him. He was not happy lately, what with how badly the search for Maximillian Turkel was going. Oh, how he was going to enjoy the interrogation process back in Colorado when he finally caught the bastard subhuman slime . . . And catch him he would, and *alive* . . . Torx had sworn that to himself and to all that he held holy that he would take the rebel alive . . .

No, that was not what troubled him.

"I thought, Knox, that it didn't make any difference *which* cells were used for a subhuman body—that each held a microcosm of the macrocosm, so to speak. The essential genetic information . . . Xs and Ys and chromosomes and such."

Tufted warts grew around Knox's deep-set eyeballs. These turned a deeper hue of purple as the mutant eyes opened wide with excitement. "But don't you see, my Lord, *this* is my discovery. It is my belief that brain cells are the secret to the mystery of why our lesser scientists cannot discover the secret to creating species of post-humans who are not sterile. However, there is a delicate process that must be used involving high-level genetic surgery and almost subatomic chromosomal manipulation. You see, it is a matter of the effect of the electrochemical processes in the gray mat—"

Torx held up a hand. "I do not need the scientific lecture, Dr. Knox. I need *results*. Do you realize the importance of this? Why, if we could create self-replicating mutants . . ."

"The Secret Conclave has worked long and hard toward that goal."

Torx slammed a fist into a hand. "We'd have the Overlord then, by his cankered balls! A group of breeding mutants will revolutionize the world—"

Suddenly, without warning, Torx sneezed violently. A prodigious amount of mucus and snot blew from his nose, landing directly in Knox's face.

Calmly, Knox drew out a linen handkerchief and wiped himself off. "Are you all right, my Lord?"

"Must be the chemicals in here. Never mind."

Torx speedily wiped his own mouth with the heel of his hand. "Where was I? Oh yes! We shall conquer this nation—a coup! And I personally shall destroy Charlemagne—perhaps with my bare hands."

"Or sneeze on him," muttered Knox under his breath.

"What?"

"Nothing, my Liege. A twitch."

Torx began to pace; the excitement of the vision coming to him elbowed even the obsession of Turkel's capture from his mind. "But most glorious of all—I had only dared *dream* of the possibilities latent here. Knox! The glorious prospect of such a world—"

"Yes! Yes, my Lord, I hate them too!"

"We will no longer need the subhumans. We can destroy each and every foul one of them! Fresh genes? They won't be needed anymore. What are you doing, Knox?"

What Dr. Knox was doing was regarding with wonder the prodigious amount of snot and mucus that he had wiped off his face. It was not worth saving his handkerchief.

"Ah, nothing, my Lord." Quickly, he stepped over and tossed the wadded, noxious cloth into a large open glass tank embedded in the tabletop.

There was a plop and a fizzing.

"What is *that*, Knox?"

"Oh—a simple little laboratory expedient I developed. It's a special acid that reduces organic matter to its component enzymes and other nutrients. By the time the acid is neutralized, it has dissolved the waste matter—and believe me, in my work, I have plenty of spare subhuman organs and whatnot lying about—into a very nice nutrient bath I can use later."

Torx grunted. "Yes. Clever. But now, you promised to show me your machines now that I have deigned to make an impromptu visit."

Actually, the hunt for Turkel was going so badly that Torx had come here to the Gamma Iowa Complex to get some of the good news that Knox had promised him. The operation was, of course, strictly undercover. Neither the Overlord nor any of his minions and sycophants knew anything of it. Even if the Overlords had gotten out of control, it *had* been the BrainGenerals who had created them, and there were a few tricks that could be used to hide information from them.

Like the very existence of the Secret Conclave . . .

Dr. Knox smiled, showing a mouthful of rotten teeth. "And that is why I have prepared the lab just for you, my Liege. If you will just turn toward my computers and observe the screens and the tanks . . ."

Clearly Dr. Knox was now in his element, and as he walked to the computer console his gait seemed more a perverse dance or caper. He tapped out numbers and messages on the keyboards, and instantly colored graphs and three-dimensional pictures appeared on the screens, accompanied by a trumpet fanfare.

"What in the name of the Booba is that?" said Torx, cocking his head as though just struck.

"Oh, just a little musical program. It gets me enthusiastic on cold winter mornings."

"Well, turn it off immediately. It's ridiculous."

"Of course, my Liege." Fingers stabbed at keys. Instantly the music halted.

"Now, then, if you'll notice the third 3-D screen from the right."

Torx turned his head. He immediately saw it: the one with the taletale coil, composed of a different color, neatly doing a little pirouette. "I've set up a model here to illustrate . . ."

"I *told* you, Knox! I don't want a lecture. I want to see results!"

"Uhm . . . well, actually, the next thing I was going to do was to show you what I'm going to do with this brain. I'm afraid the results will take the usual few weeks for vat gestation."

"But what about the previous experiments? The Conclave has been funding this operation for over a year."

"Nothing quite right, yet, I'm afraid . . . But each stab at it turns out better . . . And I thought you'd like to be here when things really click."

Torx grunted. "Yes, well . . . I trust that you are taking your victims surreptitiously."

"So much so that we haven't made even the slightest ripple of suspicion in the Network."

"You're sure?"

"You have to understand, BrainGeneral Torx . . . I am working directly with a head supervisor of the farm complex—in return for financial consideration."

"Money, bah. That's no problem. But are you sure that we can trust this fellow, this . . ."

"Brown, my Liege. Brown the Fourth, Point Six. Oh yes, of course. And he's doing an excellent job scouting out our, ah, recruits and then covering for their disappearances. The others of the complex believe that they've somehow escaped . . . As though it mattered, really. After all, they're just slaves . . ."

"It is not the subhuman scum I'm worried about, Knox."

"Of course not. At any rate, that brain there—it is that of a young female. For some reason the female cells are more conducive to my manipulation. Now then, if you could do me the great honor of bringing it over to the operating table, I can start the procedure—''

As though to illustrate his intentions, Dr. Knox hit a couple more keys. Immediately, tentacled arms containing all manner of instruments sprouted from the base of the computer. An odd robot face with huge lensed eyes slowly hove into view from the side, perched above a thicker coil like a jack-in-the-box newly sprung.

A rare smile appeared on Torx's rough lips. He enjoyed holding bloody bits of subhuman anatomy. It gave him a curious thrill . . .

He scooped the wobbly bubble of flesh and blood up in his hands, regarding it with a strange mixture of awe and glee. To think that with this hunk of gray matter they could well be at the beginning of a new mutant empire.

He would be father to a whole new civilization!

He regarded the brain in his hands for a moment and then started toward the mutant scientist.

However, he did not quite make it all the way there.

No sooner had he taken two steps than a sneezing fit came upon him. His vision went, and his path went askew. His armored shin hit a garbage pail.

BrainGeneral Torx tripped.

''Watch out! The brain—'' cried out Knox.

The brain of Hazel Larkin leaped from Torx's hands as though it still had a mind of its own. It bounced and rolled along the tabletop . . .

''No!'' cried Dr. Knox. ''Oh please, no!''

. . . and dropped directly into the tank of acid.

Much fizzing resulted as the acid immediately set to work pulling apart the organic matter.

Dr. Knox and BrainGeneral Torx stood, looking at the tank of acid in stunned silence for long moments.

Then Dr. Knox, his mottled face almost purple with apoplexy, turned to his superior. "Oh, right. That was real bright, you clumsy oaf!" Almost as soon as he'd said it, he realized his mistake. He stiffened, suddenly paralyzed with fear, waiting for a reaction. "I . . . I . . ." he stammered. Clearly his intention was to apologize, but it seemed stuck in his throat.

It is a difficult thing to maintain one's dignity while snot is running down one's nose, particularly if there is a large quantity.

Somehow, BrainGeneral Torx maintained his dignity.

With one slow deliberate move, he rubbed his metal-studded leather jacket over his nose and his mouth. He scratched himself on the lip, drawing blood, but he made no notice of this. Slowly, he lowered his arm and began walking toward Knox.

"I . . . I . . . I . . ." he tried again.

Like a striking cobra, Torx's hand shot out, grasping Dr. Knox by his throat, choking off the stream of I's. Dr. Knox gasped, his eyes growing as wide as diseased plums. Veins in his floppy head pulsed, looking as though they were about to burst from their moorings and shower the room with blood.

"If you were not so valuable to this project," said Torx through clenched teeth. "I'd kill you on the spot." After giving Knox a glare that would knock a bird out of the sky to underline his point, Torx released him.

"Yes. Yes, of course, my Liege. I was horribly out of line."

"And you were almost horribly out of *breath* as well."

"Yes."

"There is no great loss. Is it not true that there are a hundred more suitable females on the Gamma Complex?"

"Why, yes, of course."

"A brief setback. But setbacks are what make a warrior *stronger.*" Torx shrugged his shoulders with his leather gear as though tossing away whatever possible guilt in this matter lay upon them. "Besides, it was your fault. You should not maintain an atmosphere that makes a BrainGeneral sneeze, you should watch your trashcans!"

"Yes, my Liege."

"Now then. Let's see how fast that computer of yours can come up with another candidate, eh?"

"At once, BrainGeneral Torx."

Wasting no time, Dr. Knox hurried about his task.

As the mutant scientist scurried about his work, touching those keys, twisting that dial, Torx sullenly stood at repose, entering the stance of The Way, meditating upon the Conclave.

It was a secret society begun perhaps twenty years before when the BrainGenerals of the North American continent finally realized that the situation with the new Central Unit had taken an ominous twist. He had the Central Unit dubbed Charlemagne and tagged an Emperor onto that for good measure. Had they been able to, they would have simply assassinated the thing, dismantled him and his cyborg machinery and have done with it. Unfortunately, the cyborg status was far too integral to the operation of the entire network. And only a cyborg like Charlemagne could run it. If they somehow removed him and put another in his place, who knew that the new one might not be worse than his predecessor?

130

No, there had to be a plan to supplant the system with something else.

And this project was part of that plan.

A vitally important part of that plan.

He was glad he had controlled his anger. Killing Dr. Knox, as satisfying as that might have been, would have been . . . well, unfortunate.

"My Liege," said Dr. Knox. "I have the perfect replacement, culled from the files of the women of the Gamma Complex supplied by Brown."

"Yes. Excellent. So what is the bitch's name?" Already his mind was darting ahead, planning his next foray out tomorrow morning with the Bloodhounds in search for Turkel. Then he would return tomorrow and see how things progressed here.

And he would not sneeze.

"Her name, my Liege is Jennifer," said Knox, pointing up to a picture of a blond woman on the screen. "Jennifer Anderson."

CHAPTER 14

"Watch out for that branch, goddammit!"

Jack Bender looked up. Sure enough, a thick broken branch was hanging down in the path of the plane. He'd been pushing on the thing so hard that he'd forgotten to look where they were going. They changed course, directing the plane down the narrow path between the trees and out toward the flat field which Jack had found and Turkel thought would suffice as a takeoff spot.

"What's the matter?" said Turkel. "You wanna tear off the wing? You want me to stick around longer and give you hell?"

Actually, Jack wouldn't have minded that at all. They'd had a very good time last night, talking right up to Jack's curfew. Jack had to admit it to himself as soon as he woke up this morning to the predawn dark.

He was going to miss Max Turkel.

He was going to miss him a lot.

Still, he knew that keeping him around any longer would be dangerous—to Turkel, and certainly to him.

"Hell, no. I wanna get your ugly ass outta here!"

"That's the spirit, kid!" Turkel flashed him a grin full of teeth and then doubled his effort to keep the plane rolling. They were situated to either side of the fuselage, gripping handles with one hand and the ailerons with the other.

They had to stop several times to clear the path of fallen branches and rocks that, unfortunately, Jack had not noticed. But Turkel did not complain about this. He just gamely helped Jack haul the things out of the way, and then set back to work.

Theoretically, they could have started up the engine and let the prop pull the thing along. They'd already long since determined that the engine worked fine by testing it. However, Turkel didn't want to chance the propeller hitting any trees and branches and busting.

"We can fix a flat tire, kid, but that prop's absolutely priceless to me," he said.

Jack could see his point.

It took close to an hour to negotiate the path, and when they finally had the thing out, they had to rest for a while; they were exhausted.

"Hey, kid," said Turkel, slapping Jack's knee. "We had some fun last night, didn't we?"

Jack wiped sweat off his brow and nodded agreement. "Yeah, Max. You've got some pretty good stories."

Turkel had surprised him. Jack had brought along some of the corn liquor to the celebration, he'd even had some himself, but Turkel hadn't touched a drop. Said he wanted a clear head for the flight tomorrow.

"I've been around, I see some strange things, I hear some strange things."

"You *do* some strange things," Jack added.

"Yeah, well. It's a living." Turkel stood up, surveying the land. "You got the stuff all packed in the cockpit?"

"Yeah. Water, food, bandages in case you've got problems . . . the rest of the corn liquor—"

"Purely for medicinal purposes."

"Purely for medicinal purposes. Oh, and I also stuck my gun in there . . . the old .45 I showed you. And some ammunition."

Turkel's face changed. "Ah, Jack. That's a pretty thing . . . no, I couldn't take that from you. You should keep it."

"I'm probably never going to need it. You doubtless will."

"Yeah. Yeah, you're right on that. Too bad I lost all the other weapons back on that air base. Christ, I usually carry around an arsenal! I've been feeling like Casanova without his cock! Thanks, Jack." He walked away, looking out over the field. "You know, you can still come with me if you want."

"I can't."

"Just making the offer one more time. I won't razz you anymore, Jack. Maybe in fact I oughta apologize."

"Apologize for what?"

"For putting you down so much. I been way outta line on harping on the freedom thing." He once more surveyed the land. "You know, I wouldn't tell this to a soul but you—but once in a while, I miss the old farm in Salinas."

"You do?"

"Yep. Powerful stuff, knowing you have a place, a home. Awful lonesome out in the cold sometimes. This is a nice place, Jack. Maybe you do have a nice home. And you know, maybe you are free in a way."

"I am?"

"Sure. I guess the basis of freedom is having a choice. What do you call it?"

"Free will?" That's what Potts called it, when he started off on a philosophical tangent.

"Yeah. That's it. Free will. Well, you've got a choice, coming with me or staying here. And you've made that choice. So you've exercised your free will."

"Yeah." Somehow, though, Jack didn't feel very convinced.

They drank some water and then they got down to starting the plane. The engine started up like a champ, and the propeller whirred pretty as you please, and Max Turkel was all smiles.

"Say, good buddy. I'll tell you what. I been here for over two weeks now, I guess I could spare a couple more hours. You wanna go for a ride?"

Jack's eyes almost started from their orbs. "In the plane?"

"No, on my bare back. Of course in the plane, Jack."

"But . . . but someone might see us!"

"So what? No surface-to-air missiles around here. Anyway, I'll head away from the complex and keep low. We won't attract any attention."

Jack's hand involuntarily went to his neck. "My beeper node."

"Shit, you told me where the boundary is and it's *miles* away. We won't get anywhere near it."

Jack's caution was totally submerged in his over-whelming desire to fly. Even if it was for just a few minutes, and only a few hundred feet above the trees, to actually soar and dip and careen through the sea of air, *off the ground,* was something he simply could not pass up.

"Okay," he said.

"Thatta boy. Hop in. You'll be my co-pilot. It'll be just like you're doing it yourself. Shit, with those books you've been going through you probably know more about flying than I'll ever know. But nothing beats experience. Am I right?''

Jack Bender could only agree.

Eagerly he climbed into place where Turkel directed him and buckled himself in.

"Okay, Max. Let's go!"

Turkel just smiled, shook his head, and hoisted himself into the pilot's seat.

He was flying!

It was like nothing Jack Bender had ever felt before. Not like sex, eating, drinking, working, playing—all the composites of life.

He was flying!

The plane seemed to hang suspended like a kite behind the roaring motor that pulled it through the air. Max kept to his word, staying low above the tops of the trees and just circling well beyond range of the farm complex or the perimeter. Jack could not see the complex, they were so low—and he knew the people there could not see them, and *should* not see them.

Still, he longed to climb higher, higher. Go farther, *farther*. His heart thrilled as it never had before.

He was flying, and it felt as though he had been born *to fly!*

"How's it feel, kid?" said Turkel, happy as a clam himself at the prospect of his eventual soaring off and away.

"Great!"

"Thought you'd like it."

Turkel banked, and the G forces pulled at Jack's

136

heart and his soul lurched with excitement. Still, it had not been like takeoff.

God, the speed! The ecstasy as the wheels left the ground and Turkel had pulled the plane up into a steep climb!

It had been like an orgasm.

No, in some ways it was better than an orgasm, because he was in *control*. Max was right. With the controls in his hands, Jack felt as though it was *he* who was flying. And, instinctively, with that never-to-be-forgotten touch of the controls now in his inventory of mechanical skills, he knew that he could do it again, without Max.

He *knew* he could fly solo.

Laughing like a maniac, Max took the plane down in a dive and then pulled her up. The controls responded perfectly.

"Hey, kid. How come you're not screaming? That was a pretty hair-raising maneuver."

Jack wasn't screaming because he was smiling. "Do some more, Max. Teach me."

Max shrugged. "Sure. Why not? Only for a few more minutes, though. Don't wanna waste too much gas."

Max took him through the basic flying routines and showed him a few tricks. When he was straightening out from a particularly exciting roll, though, something happened.

The motor coughed.

"What's that?" asked Jack. "Is that supposed to happen?"

The propellers slowed to a standstill.

"Fuck no!" said Turkel. "Jesus Christ, Bender. I thought you said the engine was golden!"

"What can we do?"

"Well, kid," said Max Turkel, struggling with the controls as an eerie silent sound of whooshing air filled the place where the motor sound had been. "I guess we can land—or we can crash!"

CHAPTER 15

"Phil? Phil Potts?"

Phil Potts started from his absorption in his book. His hand knocked over the cup of tea, spilling it across a batch of papers on the high old-fashioned desk surrounded by slanted book stacks that looked like something from a Dickens novel. He jumped up, sending an old umbrella stand spinning, and swung around toward the voice. Jeez, was it one of the muties? Had they found his secret place in the cellar below one of the many storage barns?

But even as he swung around, tense and jumpy, he realized that the voice didn't belong to any mutant. It was a girl's voice . . . no, a woman's, soft and velvet and gentle . . . not the usual gargle or harsh racket of a mutie.

Sure enough, it was a human girl who stood there at the door (which he'd forgotten to lock, dammit) and one of his very favorites.

Jenny Anderson.

"Oh, Jenny. Really, you should have told me you wanted to come down here." That had been the condition of his revealing his secret place to her and Jack Bender—that if they wanted to come down here, they should either be *taken* down here by Phil himself, or have a definite appointment. You couldn't be too careful, if you had a hiding place—especially if, unlike Jack, who had his out in the trees, it was smack dab under the muties' noses. Actually, though, he wouldn't have been surprised if the muties knew . . . Oh, not old Brown. Brown would go bugfuck if he knew about this place. Maybe some of the others, who just didn't care. Things were pretty lax here around Gamma. From all comparisons with the other farm, factory, and government complexes that employed human slaves, the Gamma Farm C was one of the more lax. Which was all just fine with Phil Potts, since it had allowed him to sneak his collection in here. "You scared the hell out of me."

She was very pretty when she was contrite—and now, she was very contrite. Of course, she was pretty all the time. But she'd never given Phil Potts much attention.

Until now.

Now she looked like she wanted him to father her babies.

"I'm *so* sorry, Phil. But I just *had* to talk to you. It's very urgent."

"Oh. Well, come in and close that door. You never know how a voice will carry out of the barns."

"Oh, Phil, you're such a paranoid," she said, giggling, coming up to him and squeezing his arm. "No one hardly ever comes to this old place."

"Well, I'm sure glad you did, Jenny. You don't come often, and it's always with Jack."

"Oh, he's been so busy lately . . . I just don't know about Jack."

Phil Potts's ears perked up at that. "Oh?" He'd always fancied Jenny, and if Jack were out of the picture . . .

Well, maybe *he'd* have a chance with her!

"Oh, I'd rather not talk about Jack, I guess. Actually, what I came for was to borrow a book."

Phil smiled and gestured back to his shelves, stacked with books, magazines, and other odds and ends he'd smuggled in from his crooked mutant contacts in Somerville, the closest mutie town. Phil Potts's job on the complex necessitated that he have access to travel to Somerville, and so he'd been equipped with a special node that allowed him to go to Somerville, but nowhere beyond that town.

However, what the muties didn't know was that Phil had long since figured out the way to surgically remove the node. And, with the help of Jack Bender's deft hand and surgical ability, he'd removed the thing.

Now, one of these days he'd actually have the nerve to make a run for the freedom he was always talking about. Of course, if a fox like Jennifer Anderson was interested in him—well, maybe he could stick around for a while longer.

"Book? Book you say! I don't think I have any of those things!"

"Phil, don't be silly. You *will* let me borrow one, won't you?"

Phil Potts shrugged. "I let Jack borrow them all the time. Good heavens, it's thanks to me he's got the education he has. I don't know what he'd do without me."

"You know, I certainly see your value now, Phil. There's a lot I never appreciated about you that I do now." She batted her long eyelashes at him and smiled coyly. "Really."

"Gee, Jenny. That's nice to hear. I've always liked you. What kind of book do you want to borrow?"

She turned away, looking a little embarrassed. "A book about . . . well, about sex."

141

Phil's mouth immediately got very dry. "About sex?"

"Yes. You know. Lovemaking techniques. Stuff like that . . . with pictures, if you've got one."

Phil felt the blood rushing to his face. "Ah." Cripes, he was blushing like an inexperienced teen-ager, when actually he was an inexperienced twenty-two-year-old. "Sex." He turned away, looking at his piles of books. "You know, Jen, I really haven't got my books in the order I should. I'll have to, uhm . . . look through them a bit. Can you wait a day or two?"

She sighed breathily, heaving her startling breasts right in his face—or so it seemed to the agitated Phil Potts. He was suddenly very aware of the exciting scent that hung around her like a heavenly mist. "Oh well, I guess I can wait. But if you can find it for me sooner than that, Phil, you'll be my special darling."

Phil Potts felt the hair at the nape of his neck stand on end. Gooseflesh prickled along his skin, and a tingle shot up his spine. What the blazes was going on here? He was too flummoxed and flustered, though, to say much.

"I'll . . . I'll do my best, Jen. That's all I can say. I'll do my best."

"That's good enough, Phil. I'm not even going to call you Pottsie now." She leaned over and gave him a wet kiss on the forehead . . .

. . . and suddenly she had turned and was dancing away, an absolute vision of desire, melting into the darkness past the door, like a dream.

She left the door open, but Phil Potts hardly noticed. He just drifted after her in a stumbling kind of way, closed the door, and then fumbled his way back to his desk, tumbling into it, a heap of confusion and elation.

142

Could it be?

Was Jenny actually *interested* in him? Was this some kind of subtle hint that he should start making a serious play for her?

Better, were all these sexual techniques she hoped to learn intended for *him?*

The very possibility set his heart to hammering, and his brain, jacked up suddenly on hormones, unreeled a panoply of erotic scenarios.

Phil Potts stared down at the book that lay open before him. Aristotle's *Ethics.* He slammed it shut, raced over to his stacks, and desperately began tearing through his book collection looking for the book that Jenny wanted.

Finally, a book was going to get him a girl!

He, of course, *loved* books. All kinds of books. Especially since they were so rare. Human books, that was. Some of the muties read books—in fact, there was a whole mutant publishing industry to meet the reading needs of the mutie and halfsie public, complete with mutant publishers and editors. (The rumor among the human intelligentsia was that all publishers and at least some editors had been mutants long before the Final War.) However, the books were mostly trashy action-adventure novels in which brave mutants fought off monstrous rebellious uprisings from the wretched subhumans. Nothing that interested Phil Potts much.

Yes, he *loved* books, but they'd done absolutely nothing to improve his empirical love life.

Maybe, though, the tide was turning!

Phil Potts strode quickly toward the Medical Center, a dogeared and yellowed copy of Alex Comfort's *The Joy of Sex* tucked into a sweaty palm. He'd taken a few moments to peruse the pictures, unfortunately, and he'd almost literally fogged up his glasses.

The naked women all looked like Jennifer.

He turned a corner around a building and stopped so quickly he almost tripped and fell flat on his face.

Christ almighty! There was Brownie himself, standing outside the Medical Center, less than twenty yards away. Standing with him were three other mutants.

And here he was, a forbidden book in his hand, and out in the open!

Quickly, Potts raced back around the corner, hiding. He dared not go farther, lest the mutants hear his running steps. He'd have to slink away. First, though, he had to stop breathing so hard.

Mashed against the wall, telling his heart to stop sounding like a tympani drummer in a frenzy, he could not help but hear the lowered voices of the mutants.

". . . are you sure this is necessary? I mean, Dr. Knox . . . It's broad daylight!"

"I will pay you triple, Brown. You may distribute what bribes you require. But we need what we need *now!*"

"Well, it is a slow time of day. I suppose it won't cause too much commotion where she works. But you will be careful, won't you?"

"Of course."

"Uh, er, you mentioned my payment?"

Potts ventured a peek around the edge of the building in time to see a large wad of bills exchanging hands. He realized he'd never seen the mutie who was passing the money. Nor his companions, who were short and squat and looked like refugees from a body-building camp for leprous dwarfs.

144

"Thank you. I am sorry that things are not going well at Edgington Institute."

"They're going quite well, thank you," said the mutant Brownie had referred to as Dr. Knox in a wheezy voice. "We just need a new subject. Immediately."

"I can't promise I can do this again, no matter how much money you give me."

"I understand. But I think this will be the last for a while."

"Well then, gentlemen," said Brown, tucking his money into a pocket and looking around to make sure on one was watching them. Potts ducked back behind the corner just before those beady eyes were cast his way. "If you'll come this way." They started trudging away, their big feet crunching in the gravel. "Around the front. I shall make prep . . ."

And Brown's voice faded away out of Potts's earshot.

What was the meaning of all this? An exchange of bribe money . . . The Edgington Institute? And who were they talking about?

Potts had passed the Edgington Institute on his way into town. It was a big thing, just past the edge of the mutant city, with weird architecture and a certain tilty, ominous quality about it, like some of the photos that Phil had seen from early German films by such directors as Fritz Lang. The rumors were that the institute was a place where much of the local mutant genetic research took place—but why would the muties have a big research effort in the middle of Nowhere, Iowa? And besides, from what Potts could tell, the security there was pretty loose, people coming and going as they pleased.

He just couldn't figure it.

Well, here he was, with a sex book in his hand and his heart in his throat, having witnessed something odd, without knowing what it was . . . And that man called Dr. Knox. Whew, there was a weird one for you. A definite Class A scientist from the looks of those overstuffed brains.

Phil Potts seriously considered turning around and hightailing it back to his den and hiding until whatever it was that was happening blew over.

But then he looked down at the book in his hand and thought about the title, and the vision of those marvelous breasts, bare and heaving in his face, got the best of him.

He tucked the book under his shirt, straightened up, and walked toward the MedCenter. Jenny was in there; she wanted his book and maybe his body.

Jenny was going to get whatever she wanted from Phil Potts. *When*ever.

He'd been to her station before, so there was no problem finding it. However, as he walked down a sterile, medicinal corridor, a most startling thing happened.

He was suddenly confronted by the two short, muscular mutants and the man Brown had called Dr. Knox. And they were carrying a body covered by a sheet on a blanket. A female body by its outline.

"Gangway, fool!" gargled one of the mutants. "Emergency! Go!"

Automatically obeying, Potts stepped into a doorway and let the emergency party past. His nostrils cringed at the aroma peculiar to mutants as they passed him hurriedly. And he caught a glimpse of blond hair peeking from the edge of the sheet . . .

Then they were gone.

Whatever was happening, it looked pretty fishy to

Potts. But around here, as a slave, you didn't have much voice in these kinds of things. You just made a practice of looking the other way.

Now then. To Jenny. She needed that book. And maybe she needed a date, too! Did he have the nerve to ask?

When he entered her office, the first thing that Potts noticed was that Jenny wasn't there. The second thing he noticed were the papers scattered about, looking as though there had been some kind of struggle . . .

And then his self-taught logic training finally broke through the hormonal upset in Potts's brain, and he realized what had happened.

That glimpse of blond hair flashed into his mind.

"Jenny," he gasped.

And he dropped *The Joy of Sex* as he ran from the room.

CHAPTER 16

"Look, kid. There's gotta be *something* similar in the way of lines in this mishmash!"

A very disgruntled Max Turkel looked around the stacks and piles of mechanical equipment in the metallic graveyard that the mutants had accumulated over the years.

"Look, I'm telling you, Max. All you need is a clamp. The line just slipped off the gasket! I got plenty of clamps and I can fix it in a snap!"

Turkel shook his head, frowning. "Nope, Jack. I looked at that fuel line, and it didn't look good. I don't know why you used it. I don't want it fucking up again. Can't afford it. Now, are we going to start *looking* for one or are we going to stand around here with our thumbs up our asses, arguing?"

Jack Bender threw his arms up in a gesture of extreme frustration. And it had all been going so well!

Max had been able to glide the plane down to a surprisingly smooth landing in the field from which they had taken off. Jack was impressed with that. He'd taken all this very well, and when they'd found the knocked-off gas line, he'd just commented that he was damned glad he hadn't been playing with matches in the cockpit. But then he got it into his head that they needed a whole new line, not just the clamp that Jack thought necessary—and *insisted* on coming back with him to look for one.

Jack had not liked that idea at *all*.

It wasn't that Turkel coming back to the complex was *that* dangerous. Jack had brought him out a regulation jumpsuit his size, and in it the man looked like one of the heavy-machinery operators, and God knew there were plenty of *those* around here, some of which had been temporarily transferred from another complex or factory. Chances were that if he only hung around a few hours and stayed out of plain sight, the mutant supervisors wouldn't even notice him.

However, there was always the chance that they *would*. And if that happened, Jack Bender's life would immediately turn to shit.

"Ah, don't sweat it," Turkel told him. "We'll be careful. We'll be in and out, get that line, race back out here, put it in, and I will be out of your hair."

"Out of my *gray* hair," said Jack, fretting.

"Kid, your problem is you just don't know the secret of life."

"Which is?"

"Risk. Life ain't worth bupkiss if it ain't got the occasional risk in it."

"Hey, I take a lot of risks. Like you don't think I didn't put my ass on the line to help you out!"

"Look, no insult intended, guy. But let's face it— and I've been watching you on this—you're a shrewd little bastard, and each chance you take is measured down to the statistical percentile point. You're a *careful* son-of-a-bitch. And that's what I'm saying. You don't take some serious risks in your life, you don't grow. You don't change."

Jack grew surly at this. "Maybe I like myself just

149

the way I am." But he couldn't help thinking about what Jenny had said, about him *maturing*.

"Oh, yeah. You're fine, Jack. Just fine. Tell you what. Now, I got that nice little .45 you gave me up snug against my back—"

"You *what?*"

"Hey, don't split a seam. I'm a master of hidden weapons. Nobody's going to see it. Anyway, if the muties catch on to me, I'll take it out and point it at your head and say that I've been forcing you at gunpoint to do all the things you've done. And then you can elbow me in the gut, grab the gun, and be a hero. How's that?"

"That . . ." said Jack, repulsed. "That *sucks*, Turkel. We get caught, I'm accepting my responsibility in the matter. You can use the gun to try and get away. You understand?"

Turkel nodded. He did not grin, or even smile a little bit. "Sorry, Jack. I give you too much shit sometimes, you know."

"Yeah. Maybe you do."

They continued the rest of the way to the junkyard in a tense silence.

As soon as Turkel had gotten into the large barn area, though, and saw the riches of mechanical detritus, he got expansive again. "Yow! We're going to find *something* in here, that's for sure."

"Let's just hope it's a fuel line," Jack had muttered.

And now they were still looking—without a great deal of success.

"The problem is," Jack said, "we don't have any junked *planes* in here, Max. Whereas we have plenty of clamps. Look, I'll even give you extra ones and show you how to put them on if you need to."

"Right. Six thousand feet up I'm supposed to change clamps on the fucking fuel line. No, let's keep on looking. There's bound to be something comparable in this mess."

They were still looking when the door slammed open and someone ran into the barn behind them. Jack was so surprised he almost jumped out of his boots. Turkel stayed cool, though. He just swiveled and began reaching for the gun stuck in the back of his belt.

"Jack! Jack, thank God, there you are!"

Jack put a hand toward Turkel. "It's okay, Max. He's a friend."

Max relaxed.

Standing there by the open door was Phil Potts, heaving exhausted breaths, looking as though he'd just seen his own ghost. "Jack . . . Jack . . . It's Jenny . . ."

"Jenny? What about Jenny?"

Abruptly, Phil noticed Turkel. He did a double take.

"Hi there," said Turkel. "Acme Mechanical Device Recovery. Got any broken transistor radios?"

Phil Potts blinked. His mouth fell open. "I know you!"

"Pottsie—Jenny. What about Jenny? What—" Jack looked from Potts to Turkel and back again. "You *know* him?"

"Yeah! That's . . . that's Maximillian Turkel! The famous Human Liberation freedom fighter."

"Do I have to kill the guy now?" said Turkel, reaching back for the gun.

"No, no! You don't understand. You're my *hero*! I'm a real fan of yours."

"You are?"

"What about Jenny, Phil?"

"Yes, yes, yes!" Phil stepped forward, grabbed Turkel's hand, and pumped it heartily. "Wow, what a guy. Did you really blow up that chemical factory single-handed without hurting any human beings?"

"Yeah. That was me. One of my best—But hey, how do you know about me, Putzie, or whatever your name is."

"I get *all* the underground papers. Your picture had been in there a few times. Lots of stories about you. And hey, the last I heard, the muties are throwing everything they can in an effort to find you after that Kansas air base fiasco . . . and . . . Oh dear. You're here and . . . Jeez!"

Phil Potts finally shut up.

"Potts, for the love of God, tell me whatever you have to tell me about *Jenny,* before I have to slap you!"

"Jenny? Oh, yes, Jenny. The muties took her down to this genetic testing place against her will. You know, Jack, if we get caught with Maximillian Turkel, we're dog food!"

"A genetic testing . . . Jenny . . . But why . . ."

"Yeah. I'm pretty sure they kidnapped her. Looked like she put up a struggle in her office, too. I think that Brown had something to do with it. He took money from this really twisted-looking mutie dork named Dr. Knox. He had—"

"Knox . . . Yes . . . I saw them talking the other day. I thought something strange was going on with those two. But why would they—"

And then realization flooded through Jack Bender.

The disappearance of Hazel Larkin, the supposed escapes of the other human complex workers . . . and now Jenny. God, it all tied together into a horrible web.

And at the middle of it was a fat, ugly mutant spider named Brown.

"What place did you say they took her to, man?" said Turkel, immediately taking charge, apparently having the same realization as Jack.

"I didn't. They said it was the Edgington Institute. I pass it going into town sometimes."

"How do you know the muties do genetic research there?" Turkel pressed on.

"I don't. I've never been inside. That's just the scuttlebutt about the place I hear from my contacts."

"Any hint at all as to what the nature of these experiments is?"

"No."

Jack was shaking his head. "They never come back."

"What?" said Turkel.

"The people that have been disappearing. They never come back." Fear mixed with anger and desperation filled him. "We've got to do something."

"Well, I figured you should know," said Potts. "I'll do whatever I can."

"Thanks, Phil. I appreciate it."

"Can you fix the plane yourself, Max? I have to go and get Jenny." He could barely hold back the tears. "I can't help you anymore, till I get her back."

"Hey yo! Hold your horses there, guy. You're not the rebel commando around here. I am. So I think it would be well advised for you to accept my assistance in this business."

"Uh, uh, Max. It's too much of a chance for you to go running off to Somerville."

"Shit, kid. Didn't you hear me going on and on about risk? Shit, I've got a little bit of real *livin'* before me today, and I'm looking forward to it."

"Max, I can't allow—"

"Shut up, Jack. You helped me. I'll help you. Beside, I can't stand the thought of those warped mutie hands on that pretty little girl. Better even *my* degenerate paws than a mutie's!"

Jack had no quick comeback for that. He was too absorbed in thought, too distracted. Jenny! The bastards had Jenny! "You'll take us there, Phil."

"Sure. One major problem, though, Jack," said Phil Potts, looking truly concerned for the first time. "Your neck marker node. If you go beyond the periphery, the lights will light up on the mutie's control board like a Christmas tree."

"Yeah. I was just thinking about that." Jack fingered his neck thoughtfully, feeling the hard implant. "Well, there's nothing else to do then."

"What? You mean just Mr. Turkel and I are going?" said Phil, looking decidedly nervous at the prospect.

"No," said Jack grimly. "It means that, somehow, we're going to have to dig the sucker out."

CHAPTER 17

The Bloodhound was taking a leak.

The mutant canine-cum-humanoid-cum-cyborg creature had raised its leg, and a jet of greenish-yellow liquid gushed out and onto the fencepost, streaming down into a puddle. Its half-plastoid, half-flesh face was bent in an expression of pleasure and release.

Suddenly, the radar web atop its head quivered. The monstrous, batlike ear twitched with incoming sensory data. The huge, striated flat nose sniffed and ruffled.

The large, dark eyes opened and looked up. A whimper escaped its caninelike mouth.

"What," said BrainGeneral Torx, "are you doing, Bloodhound 00A49?"

The tone of the voice was such that the three-hundred-pound creature immediately cut off the flow of its urine.

"Peeing, sir."

"We are not out in the woods. Did I give you permission to relieve yourself in such a manner?"

The Bloodhound shivered contritely, shrinking away from its master. "No, sir," it whined.

Without warning, Torx unleashed a kick of his hard and heavy metal-studded boot into the creature's posterior, sending him scurrying off, his plastoid signal tail between his legs. "Then find an uncivilized place to pull your nonsense then!"

Foul son-of-a-bitch-oid! thought Torx as he straightened his disheveled leather jacket and turned to his current secondary officer. "Morkern!"

"Yes, sir," said the military mutant, executing a perfect march step to be within respectful distance of his commanding officer. Lieutenant Morkern was a Class H mutant, especially created to be lieutenants in armed services. Morkern, as all Class Hs tended to be, was thin with a baby face and a brown nose.

"Lieutenant Morkern, take a note. When this death hunt is through, I wish to have all Bloodhounds under my command taken in for house-training programming. We are on a Fellow's property. Bloodhounds should be able to distinguish between the woods and private property."

"Yes, sir. Noted. It will be done."

"Good. Now then, you say that this Fellow has a lead."

"Yes, sir. It came in this morning."

"Excellent. For all the good the Bloodhounds are doing us, we may as well have let them remain in their electrokennels chewing their kibble."

"Yes, sir."

"Well, don't just stand there! Knock on the door!"

"Yes, sir." The lieutenant hustled up the walkway to the house.

Actually, Torx could see, it was more a *cottage* than a house. For one thing, it wasn't very large, and for another it looked decidedly un-American—more like something you might find in the English countryside. Its roof was thatched, and the dry stuff oozed comfortably over the ramshackle wood frame like a floppy cap. There were flower pots in the window

156

boxes, filled with daffodils and tulips contributing to the wonderful smell of the garden and the grass in front of the house. All contributed to the feeling of a comfortable, snug, living quilt pulled over a comfortable, drowsy existence.

BrainGeneral Torx hated it. The whole atmosphere clashed with everything severe in his soul, his training, his religion.

Moreover, something about the whole scene made him feel distinctly uneasy.

He had seen places like this—and the creatures who'd lived in them.

Lieutenant Morkern leaned over and knocked on the small, round-topped doorway.

"Yes?" a voice said sleepily from inside.

"BrainGeneral Torx and company request an audience."

"Ah, yes! Because of my report. Of course! Just a second! Just a second!" There were clumping sounds from inside. When the door unlatched, a short creature wearing half-frame glasses peered out into the daylight, blinking.

Torx almost lost his composure. He ground his teeth and his nostrils flared and a grumbling started deep down in his gut, like heavy machinery digging into stubborn clay.

It was a fobbit!

Torx could not believe his eyes. He *hated* fobbits and all their ilk out in the unclassified zone of posthumans. In his religion of The Way, these were considered unwashed creatures, almost as bad as the subhumans.

The fobbit was a short, perfectly formed man with side whiskers and a twinkle in his eye. He wore a checked waistcoat and a floppy purple bowtie. Below his baggy woolen pants, his feet were bare—and around the side of those feet and tufted on the toes were a generous helping of hair.

The fobbit took a large meerschaum pipe from his mouth and smiled at his company through a bushy set of whiskers. "Ah! You have come, no doubt, to ask about my report of yesterday! Welcome, welcome. My name is Harpo the Fifth. Point Nine, if you want to get technical—and from the looks of you, you do."

During the fifty years of escalating mutant wars, some human scientists naturally saw that mutated human DNA structure need not emerge as horrible monsters programmed for death and destruction. A whole community, in fact, worked on what they dubbed "beneficial strains" of mutants. One faction, particularly enamored of fantasy literature, created mutant types modeled on idealistic forms of the human archetype.

Thus were born such creatures as fobbits—benevolent creatures accepted by mutant leaders now as brothers, and yet forced to live among the halfsies because the main lot of war-mad mutant strains from A to Z could not stomach the treacly *niceness* of the things.

Indeed, BrainGeneral Torx found his stomach turning even as he stared down at the fobbit now.

Still, the awful creature had information that he needed, and so should be treated with some cordiality.

"It makes no difference," he barked, maintaining his civility with difficulty. "But we need not dawdle. My lieutenant informs me that you have information for us."

"Oh, yes! But won't you have a spot of tea! And I've baked up some delicious blueberry crumpets.

Along with fresh butter, they'll make a splendid treat. I can just bring them out right now, and we'll have a splendid snack!''

"The plane, mister," ground Torx.

"The plane!" echoed Lieutenant Morkern.

"Ah, yes, the plane!" Suddenly Harpo's attention was distracted by the snarling passage of a Bloodhound. "My . . . what interesting beasties you have there. Quite a few of them, too, from the looks of them.''

"Do not change the subject," demanded Torx. "You answered the inquiry posted in the papers concerning a certain type of plane that may have passed here two weeks ago.''

"Yes! And you promised a reward, too. I have some serious work to do in the backyard garden, and that money would go a long way . . .'' The fobbit suddenly blinked beneath his half frames and stared out again at the canine creatures sniffing around in the distance. "My word, though. Come to think of it . . . Aren't those *Bloodhounds?* My goodness, the horrible things I've heard about those creatures. Oh dear.'' The fobbit's hands nervously twittered at his pipe. "Does this mean that you're tracking some poor human?''

"Yes," said Torx, not one for niceties. "Tell us about the plane.''

"The *plane,*" echoed Morkern, trying to look threatening but failing.

"I . . . I'm sorry. But if this information is meant to be used to *harm* somebody, I couldn't possibly . . .''

"If it's what we want, we'll pay you double," snarled Torx.

"You'd best not fool with my leader," said Morkern with great gravity. "He's a BrainGeneral.''

"Oh . . . dear. I wondered why you were wearing that ludicrous outfit. Well . . . No, I could have used the money, but I'll not contribute information so that your sort can visit genocide upon the founding zygotes."

"What did you say?" said BrainGeneral Torx.

"Sacrilege!" cried Lieutenant Morkern. "The subhumans are the preliminary gametes. It is the after races who are the true and holy zygotes!"

"No, no, I don't care about that. It's that the little fool won't tell us about the plane!"

"Yes!" said the fobbit defiantly, backing off. "Now if you gentlemen will just excuse me, I'll bid you a good day." Harpo stepped back behind the doorway and prepared to close the quaint door.

BrainGeneral Torx lunged.

A single gloved hand caught Harpo by the front of his shirt and hefted him up to Torx's eye level. The meerschaum tumbled down to crack on the flagstones below, spreading ashes and tobacco.

"Tell me about the plane," spat Torx. "Or *die!*"

"Yes, tell him about the plane, or die a horrible death!" screeched Morkern, getting excited.

"Shut up, Morkern." Torx shook the fobbit and repeated his threat.

"No!" said Harpo the fobbit. "You cannot do this! I am a citizen. I have rights. I am protected by the law!"

"When I am in the area, fool, I *am* the law," Torx said. "The plane."

"Help! Help me! Good neighbors! Someone! Anyone! Assault, rape, holocaust!"

Torx turned to Morkern. "Summon the 'Hounds."

"Yes, sir." Morkern drew out a small device from his back pocket and pressed a stud. Instantly, there was a yapping from the roaming Bloodhounds. Within seconds, all six of them had hurtled the fence and stood around the confrontation like an audience eager to participate. Razor-sharp jaws snapped and oil drool slathered down to destroy whole clumps of picture-perfect grass and garden.

"Have a sniff there, Fido X911," said Torx, swinging the captive Harpo the fobbit over to the nearest canine.

The Bloodhound began to snuffle at the creature's crotch. Then, excited, it opened its jaws. Just before they snapped closed, however, Torx yanked the interrogant away from the beast.

"You see," Torx said in a conversational tone of voice. "Bloodhounds are far worse than you can possibly imagine."

Harpo looked about on the nether borders of fobbit sanity. "Very well! Very well! I will tell you!" he gasped.

"And it had better be the truth, or we shall let the 'Hound have your silly carcass."

"Yes, yes! I shall tell the truth. Two weeks ago, I was up very early. Planting. I heard a roar. I looked up. It was the plane described in the article. Down to the registration number on the bottom."

"And which way was it headed?"

"I haven't finished. Bear with me, if you want the whole story. The plane was coughing."

"Coughing."

"It was making strange noises. As though the engine was in trouble. And it was descending! Quickly!"

"What! Fobbit!" said Torx, with growing excitement. "Which way was it descending?"

"That way!" said Harpo weakly, pointing. "Northwest."

"Toward the Gamma Farm Complex?"

"Yes. Toward the Gamma Farm Complex. Now, will you please call off those foul beasts. And then lower me to the ground. I'm barely able to breathe."

BrainGeneral Torx's mind reeled.

Close! Maximillian Turkel's plane had gone down so *close!*

But that had been two weeks ago—could Turkel still be in the area? Torx had to know. He would search every inch of the place—if Turkel had been wounded, as the report had said he was, then the chances were that he was still in the area, recovering.

And he would be Torx's!

"BrainGeneral! Please," said the dimunitive creature.

Torx let him down, and as he did so the Bloodhounds converged upon him. Huge muscles strained against their flanks, and the sharp jaws snapped like unleashed bear traps. They had their nostrils full of the scent of meat, and their bloodshot eyes bulged with ravenous frenzy.

"And call off these 'Hounds, for mercy's sake."

Torx's mouth quirked. "Has the squadron been fed yet today, Morkern?"

"Why, no, sir. You were the one who said a little edge of hunger sharpened their senses."

Torx spun on his heel and started walking down the flagstones. "A little meal won't hurt them."

"Yes, sir!" said Morkern, touching the appropriate button on the control device. "Sic 'im, boys!"

"No!" screamed the fobbit. "Nooooo!

Soothed by the music of tearing flesh and breaking bone and the choked-off screams of Harpo the fobbit,

BrainGeneral Torx hastened down the walkway toward what he was convinced was a stepping-stone to his destiny.

Maximillian Turkel!

In his very marrow, he felt that Maximillian Turkel was to be his, this very day!

CHAPTER 18

He was flying.

Jack Bender was flying through a storm. Wind and rain buffeted the plane, and hailstones beat against the cockpit window.

The plane suddenly began to dive.

He could feel the tremendous G forces against his chest and face.

He reached down to the controls to steady the plane, to bring it back into steady flight . . . and suddenly he realized that he'd totally forgotten how to fly.

"Max," he said, turning to his co-pilot. "Max, you have to help me! I've forgotten how to fly!"

He looked over to the other seat.

The seat was empty.

He was alone! All alone!

The plane dived down and down into a mass of clouds. Lightning smashed through them like sudden strobes . . .

And deep in the clouds, rearing up like a dark menace, was a gigantic face. A mutant's face. From long ago . . . very long ago . . .

And in the midst of his fear and his terror, Jack Bender realized he had seen that face before . . .

"Jack. Jack! Hey kid, what's going on? You can't come with us like that."

Consciousness flowed like water into an almost-empty tank. "Huh?"

"You fainted, kid."

"I did. Why?"

"Cripes, we might as well have used a *general* anesthetic." Jack recognized Max Turkel's voice. "Like a baseball bat to the back of the head."

"Well, we *did* get it out," said Phil Potts, holding up a gory collection of metal and plastic, wire leads dangling down like ganglia of some artificial brain. "And he is still alive."

Jack remembered.

He looked around. There were the mirrors set up around him so that he could help in the procedure. His fingers drifted up to his neck, found the slick residue of blood, the tight knot of stitches on his throat.

The tracker node . . .

They'd gotten it *out!*

"I don't feel so good," he said, woozily dropping back into the chair. It wasn't every day that you operated on yourself, especially after two weeks of continued stress. Nonetheless, behind the pain in his neck and the woozy nausea churning about in his gut was a tremendous sense of *release* that almost canceled out the ill feeling.

"You're gonna be okay, Jack. You did just great," said Max, gripping his arm in a supportive, almost fatherly fashion. "Now, Phil here's going to give you that pep hypo you brought me but never used. It'll kill the pain and give your corpuscles a cup of coffee."

They were in Phil's basement. Jack remembered now—Max had run out and gotten the first aid sack at the tree hut, while he and Phil had fixed up the

165

impromptu operating stand . . . the same they had used when he'd helped Phil dig his node out. It had been a lot harder working on himself, but Max's hands had proved amazingly steady with scalpel and forceps, and they'd managed to nick no veins and, thank God, avoid the carotid. Thank God the muties still considered their human slaves so dumb—they could easily have made the nodes much harder to extract. But as there had been practically no history of humans doing it, they apparently assumed that the precautions in tracker placement were sufficient.

Still, the whole procedure had been a bitch.

But he'd *had* to. There was no question about that. He'd *had* to get the sucker out, so that he could go and rescue Jenny.

And it had to be done fast.

Turkel jabbed the hypodermic into Jack's arm, pushed down the plunger easily and steadily, shooting him up with the drug mixture. The man's whole attitude during the procedure was one of profound competence. Clearly, Max Turkel knew something of battlefield medicine, and that helped both him and Phil Potts tremendously through the surgery.

Almost immediately, the pain eased. A speedy rush followed soon after, and Jack Bender felt not only human again, but absolutely wired and ready for action.

"How long was I out?"

"Only a couple of minutes."

"Then it's what . . . still afternoon?"

"Right."

"I say we go now instead of when it gets dark."

"You gonna be okay, kid?"

"Just bring another hypo of that stuff, and I'll be great."

166

"Potts? You okay with that?"

"I don't know . . . There's a lot of mutants running around about now. Three humans are going to stick out like sore thumbs. I say we wait at least until six. That's only . . . what . . . an hour and a half away?"

"Yeah. That sounds good to me."

"But Jenny . . ."

"Look, Jack. You've just enlisted yourself into the Warrior's School of Hard Knocks. I'm going to have to give you a crash course in Reality 101. Chances are if they're going to do anything nasty to your girl, they've already done it by now. And if they haven't, an hour or so ain't going to make much difference. Potts here is right. I don't care what kind of disguises we've got, we're not going to be able to get into a mutant research center with a lot of muties around. And we're sure as hell not going to do Jenny any good if we're *dead,* now are we?"

"So what are we going to do then!" said Jack, his concern and fear for Jenny constricting into a tight knot below his rib cage. He got up to his feet, but immediately a wave of dizziness forced him to sit back down.

"For one thing, you can start by recovering." Turkel slapped Potts on the shoulder. "In the meantime, Phil and I are going to get this crazy assault thing together. Aren't we, my new and well-read friend!"

Phil Potts looked as though he were peering over a steep cliff and was experiencing a sudden attack of vertigo.

"Uhm, yeah, Max. Whatever you say."

Jack Bender closed his eyes and concentrated on getting his shit together.

He had to get Jenny *out* of there.

He had to . . . or he knew he'd never see her again.

CHAPTER 19

Jenny Anderson bit one of her captors.

The mutant's screech of pain did her heart good; the creature's rancid taste didn't.

"Yeoow!" said the short, muscle-bound mutant. As much in reaction as anything else, he pushed the woman away from him against the wall. "The bitch bit me!" He pulled a meaty fist up into the air, cocked to deliver a blow to her face.

The other mutant, who could have been his twin, grabbed the arm before it could deliver any harm, though. "Stop! We shall do her no damage. Knox specified no damage, especially to the head!"

"But she bit me!"

Jenny spat with pure contempt. "And I'm already *sorry* for it."

"Quiet! Why are you struggling?" said the calmer of the mutants—the one who hadn't been bitten. "You are in bonds! You can go nowhere! What, do you think it is possible to escape us?"

Jenny considered this. Yes, that was true enough. From the moment she'd woken up in this room, the fumes of the ether still clinging to her mind, she'd been handcuffed, with shackles on her ankles for good measure. And it wasn't as though she knew where she was either—where would she go if she escaped, anyway? Nonetheless, she'd bitten the mutant anyhow. Why?

Because he'd gotten close enough and because she *felt* like it.

The only thing that Jenny Anderson was pretty sure about was that she wasn't in the Gamma Complex anymore. She figured that because of her neck.

There was something weird about the area where the tracker node was, and Jenny figured that somehow these mutants and their bosses had nullified it. Did this mean that her kidnapping had been with the blessing of the supervisors? If so, then why had it been done in such a slipshod fashion? Hijacking her right out of her office! Really!

But once she got over her indignation, and Jenny began to give this business some serious thought, she added the situation up and she remembered those disappearances of the past few months, the last of which had been Hazel Larkin.

All people who had disappeared for good.

And that was when Jenny got a little scared and a little mean, precipitating the bite. At least now she knew that they weren't supposed to harm her—for the moment. But why were they supposed to be particularly careful with the head?

What was it about her head that was so important? Jenny didn't have a good feeling about this business at all—she didn't think what they were after was her charming personality.

"What's going to happen to me?"

The good-looking mutant—the one with his nose not half chewed off—leered. "You don't want to know, sweetheart."

"Anyway, we can't tell you," said the other. "It

might permanently damage your delicate mental health.''

They both laughed.

Jenny Anderson didn't like the sound of this at all. She realized that she could do one of two things, and since she realized she wasn't particularly disposed toward tears, she cursed them.

They laughed again, enjoying themselves.

"Better sit down and have a rest, subbie," said Half Nose. "You're going to need it where you're going."

Which did not raise bright prospects in Jenny's mind. She slumped against the wall and slid down to a crouch, while her guards walked over out of earshot and conversed in low tones.

It was slowly dawning upon Jenny Anderson that this might be *it*. That she was going to die. She was only eighteen years old and she hadn't thought much about death. You *lived* first, and then you died, right? Hers had been a fairly sheltered existence, and even though Phil Potts would bring the subject up from time to time, in philosophical terms, of course, she'd never discussed it. She had to *live,* have children, and then she'd get ready to pass on to whatever was next on the list.

The muties had let their human slaves keep their religions, but encouraged the practice of a supremely obeisant form of Christianity similar to that of the blacks in the South in the nineteenth century. This faith put stock in faithfulness, obedience, and, most importantly, pie in the sky when you die, because there's not much here on Earth. Actually, Jenny Anderson had always been reasonably satisfied with her lot on Earth. She'd mouthed the prayers that her caretakers had taught her, but not thought a great deal

171

about them. Of *course* if there was a male God up there looking down on a troubled Earth he'd love Jenny Anderson. *Everybody* loved Jenny Anderson . . . she was so cute and perky. Even a lot of the mutants who openly disdained subhumans seemed to go out of their way to be nice to pretty Jenny.

Now, though, when it seemed as though things were not quite as rosy for her continued existence as she had thought only hours ago, she decided that she'd better talk to God for a bit and let Him know that He'd better have a nice room with pink curtains all ready for her if she was going to die.

And a handsome boyfriend. Definitely a handsome boyfriend . . .

Of course, she'd miss Jack terribly. And the thought of Jack—who'd never know what had happened to his beloved, caused a few tears to drip from Jenny's eyes.

"Ah ha! The bitch realizes the seriousness of her dilemma," observed one of the mutants. "It is good when the subhumans clearly know their place."

"Wait a minute," said the other. "I have a message coming over." The creature had a radio implant grafted onto his large earlobes and he reached up to adjust a vernier, listening intently. "Yes, brother. They are ready for her. We must bring her into the lab now."

"Come, bitch. Your destiny awaits you."

And when he reached for her, Jenny bit him again.

"What is this!" said Dr. Knox, pointing to the bruise on the side of Jenny Anderson's face. "I thought I told you, don't hurt her and most especially, don't harm her head!"

"She fell."

"I didn't fall. They hit me," said Jenny, glaring at

172

her attacker. "Hard. Feels like a concussion. Yes, a bad concussion. Maybe you'd better just forget about using me, huh, doctor?"

Dr. Knox just shook his wobbly head wearily. "I shall deal with you two later. But it looks as though the female is in proper condition."

"We told you we'd take good care of her."

"Yeah," said the other, stepping forward to upstage his fellow. "And *I* didn't hit her, doctor."

"The time for rewards and punishment is not now. Please, just put her up on the examination table."

"Where we put the other one?"

"Shall we take her clothes off?"

Dr. Knox went to his control board. "Yes, yes. The same procedure."

"But, doctor. This one is *conscious* . . . and she bites."

"What, have I two *dunces* for assistants? Do what is necessary to prevent harm to yourselves. But what is your problem? After all, the subhuman *is* tied up!"

The two short mutants looked at each other. "You hold her head while I remove her clothing."

"No," said the other. *"You* hold her head while *I* remove her clothing!"

"Silence! Norn, you hold her head. Clack, you remove her clothing," roared the doctor, losing his patience. "Carefully, do you hear?"

Their bickering cut off, the two mutants obeyed.

First they hefted Jenny up onto a flat examination table. Then, without removing her bonds, while the creature called Norn held a grip on Jenny's head, Clack tied ropes around her ankles and wrists. Then, while Norn continued his hold (and a firm one it was—Jenny could barely move her head), Clack went

173

to a drawer, pulled out a scalpel, and proceeded to slowly cut Jenny's clothes from her body.

By now Jenny was beginning to feel fear's icy fingers clutching at her heart. And it wasn't so much the gleaming razor, slicing off her clothing bit by bit, revealing first her breasts, then her abdomen, then her hips, until she was completely naked upon the table . . .

It was the leer of pure enjoyment upon the mutant's hideous face that almost made her lose it.

And the speck of drool, dripping from its mouth.

"Not bad," said Norn. "Not bad at all."

A freeze of sexual terror swept through Jenny. She did not think that mutants had any prurient interest in human flesh, but when Norn released her, she said, "I must warn you, I have a terrible sexual disease."

"Oh, good," said Clack. "Even better! Doctor, can we have the body when you are through?"

"We'll see," said the doctor, not even looking up from his controls.

The short, muscular mutants left.

"What . . . what are you going to do?" stammered Jenny, her relief at the departure of the mutant guards melting rapidly as she turned and looked at all the gleaming machinery—and realized how cold it was in here without any clothes on.

"A moment . . ." said Dr. Knox. "There." He pressed a button.

A machine connected to a coil detached itself from the wall, swimming before her like a vision in metal. It was a mockery of a humanoid face, with a grille for a mouth, a nose . . . and huge eyes, distorted by lenses.

"Now then," said a tiny voice from the grille. "First, some questions . . ."

Metal and plastic tentacles with scalpels and hypos for tips sprouted around her like the garden of some demented doctor.

CHAPTER 20

It was still light outside, but Phil Potts had determined that since it was after six o'clock, the mutant activity would have died out in the area of Somerville where they had to go.

The party struck out, armed and determined, for the Edgington Institute.

Jack Bender wore a flesh-colored bandage around his neck, with his collar up high to hide the recent surgery. It would not do to have any mutants see that this was a human who had somehow removed his tracker node. That would instantly identify him. No, Potts had supplied them with the gray jumpsuits that workers from the complex who were permitted into town used. Hopefully, they would attract little undue attention.

Security was not strict, for simple reasons. The regular complex workers had everything they needed on the farm, from work and food to recreation. They simply had no particular reason to want to venture out even if they could—and besides, they had been thoroughly indoctrinated against it.

Even Jack Bender felt a little funny as he walked past the blinking markers delineating the periphery. He'd never been this far out before . . . And though he'd occasionally fantasized about seeing the world, it had only been just that . . . a fantasy. Actually embarking on a journey out of his normal living space was somehow *jarring* to his sense of normality. True, the trees along the side of the road that led to the town were the same; indeed, it was as though he were simply walking in a reflection of his home environment. But when the team crested the small rise that lay between the Gamma Complex and Somerville, that was when Jack Bender's mind was truly tilted.

And it was then, not when he crossed the line, that he realized that he had done it.

He was off the complex.

He was away from the place where he had been born and where he thought he'd die. In his nightmares, he'd always expected the experience to be traumatic, like a child tugged untimely from its mother's womb. Instead, however, he felt *exhilarated*.

It was a shame they could not have taken a vehicle, but Somerville was not a long walk. Besides, any kind of vehicle would have attracted undue attention to three humans so close to a fairly classified area.

Somerville itself was a throwback to older times. Most towns had survived the Final War between the mutants and humans, and like them, Somerville was fairly intact. It was a mid-sized town with churches and a city hall and a downtown section that had glittered with neon and the pallor of misuse. But cast over it all now, as with all the other formerly human-run towns, was the aura of *strange*, the shiver and warp of *mutation*. Things seemed slightly bent, like a Salvador Dali painting. Where there should have been just straight normal architecture, there was an overlay of strange scaffolding and ornamentation with a blend of clashing colors. The cityscape was like an old picture, perverted and drawn by a madman.

However, if the town of Somerville was covered by an overlay of mutation, then the Edgington Institute was the pure and unsullied reality. Hardly the normal blocky architecture of the previous century, it was rather a conglomeration of cubes and squares and other geometric forms, connected by catwalks and sprouting alien cupolas, spires, and antennae.

"Yep," said Max Turkel matter-of-factly. "That's a mutie-spawned building all right. So long, Frank Lloyd Wright!"

"Huh?" said Jack.

"A famous twentieth-century architect," said Phil. "He was best known for his—"

"Okay, okay, lectures later," said Turkel. *"Everything* later. First we have to get one Jennifer Anderson out of the Hospital from Hell there."

"Right," said Jack, snapping himself out of his alarm at seeing the building. "You're the leader here, Max. I think you've done this kind of thing a few more times than Phil and I have."

He could not take his eyes off the institute. He was used to seeing the twisted and grotesque variation on the humanoid perpetrated by the mutants. But he'd only seen plain vanilla farm buildings before. Looking at this strange structure brought him the full shock of the new, and Jack was sure he wasn't at all comfortable with what these angles and contortions of steel and plastic and wood spelled.

Quite simply, a rebellion away from anything warm and human about life into the purely *alien.*

"Okay, kid. You want it, you got it. Phil, hand me those binoculars you so conveniently dug up."

Phil did so.

"There's a good lad. What would we have done without you?"

"I don't know. Thanks to me, we all have guns and equipment, and we know that the muties have Jenny." Phil was a little white about the gills though—despite his excellent contributions (especially the .45 automatics and ammunition, which he'd gotten through his underground and intended to use if and when he escaped from the complex), he clearly didn't look totally comfortable with this whole business. Still, he was along, and he plainly knew how to use his weapon. These were the things that counted.

Max grunted, squinting into the lenses. "And thanks to you, we also know a little bit about this here institute. Tell me, Phil. What have you observed about the security precautions there?"

Phil shrugged. "Well, I've seen guards by the gate."

"Yep. There's the gate. But I don't see any guards."

"Is that good or bad?" asked Jack.

"Dunno. Could be either. Could be we've got a free stroll to the front door. Could be we've got a force field."

"Force field."

"Uh huh. Don't often find the suckers, 'cause they take a hell of a lot of power expenditure to operate, but they're a bitch to bust through." He lowered the glasses, handed them back to Phil. "Well, there's only one thing for it. We go and check it out. Are we ready?"

"Oh, yes," said Jack. "Jenny's in there."

"Maybe you'd better not ask me that question," said Phil.

"Okay," said Max grimly. "Question withdrawn. Let's do it men. Let's show 'em that humans still can pack a wallop!"

"That your rebel pep talk?" said Phil. "I thought you, like, gave a real long speech about freedom and individuality and stuff."

"There's no time," said Jack. "Besides, I've already heard it."

Max grunted. "Yeah, well, just try to shoot straight, kid, huh? That's all I ask."

They marched down to the gate.

As Max had ascertained through his binoculars, there were no guards. For all the strangeness of the building, the gate was mundane enough, including a booth for the nonexistent guard to sit in. And there was no telltale hum or electronic shivering of a force field.

Max looked around, scratching his jaw. "Hmm. Maybe they went for a pee. Or for some coffee and doughnuts."

"Maybe for both."

"I don't know, guys. I don't like it." Max looked around suspiciously. "Me, I like moving into mutant territory by stepping over a dead mutant body."

"I could do without that," said Phil, nervously holding his gun under his arm.

"I don't care," said Jack. "I just want to get Jenny."

"Here we go then. C'mon, double time." They ran around the gate barrier and into the front yard of the institute toward what looked to be the front door.

Almost as soon as they passed the line, however, an alarm rang.

"Well, so much for going in quietly," said Max.

A monotone voice began to announce from hidden speakers. "Alert! Unauthorized subhuman intruders. Alert! Unauthorized subhuman intruders. Armed and presumed dangerous!"

"Christ! Fucking sophisticated technology."

"What can we expect?" said Jack, stepping up his pace, bringing out his gun fully. Now that the bastard knew he had it, there was no sense in hiding it.

"Oh, laser beams," said Max. "Grenades, rocket launchers. A messy and grisly death. Stuff like that."

"Wonderful," said Phil.

A uniformed mutant with four arms, each holding a different weapon, raced from the door, screaming. "Halt! Halt villains!"

"Shee-it," said Max, raising his gun and blasting the thing. The .45 mm slug, a dumdum, tore through the mutant's long nose cartilage, slammed into its brain, and exited the back of the cranium, carrying no little amount of blood and gray matter with it. The mutant crumpled to the cement, twitching and spasming out the rest of its life.

Max Turkel, smiling, stepped over the thing. "Ah, I feel much better." He looked down at the thing, perusing its armament. "Ah ha. What have we got here? Why, it's a machine gun! And it's *not* an AK-47. Let's just see—"

He bent down to pull the thing out of the creature's cooling hand.

"Max! Watch out!" cried Jack.

There was another of the four-armed things coming out from the door. Jack took a quick shot at the thing, but the bullet went wide, smashing out a pane of glass behind it.

However, casually as you please, Max Turkel grabbed the machine gun, swung around, and strafed a hail of bullets, smashing more glass and almost cutting the thing in two.

"Weapons galore, guys," said Turkel. "Take your

181

pick. Nicely oiled Uzi here. Actually works decently.''

"I think I'll stick with what I kinda know," said Jack.

"Me too," echoed Phil.

"Ah, c'mon. These things are Class P's. Mutant samurais. Look at the nice swords they got. Take the swords, guys, at least. For me.''

Jack nodded, deferring to Max's command position. Looking down at the dead and gory mutant, he saw that, indeed, in its lower right hand was a sleek, sharp-bladed sword. He grabbed it by his left hand and stood again, seeing that Phil had taken up the other fallen mutant's sword.

"That's it," said Turkel, a strange kind of excitement invading his eyes. "Now, c'mon, let's go rip these guys another set of assholes!"

They moved into the Edgington Institute warily, Max Turkel with his Uzi first.

As soon as they stepped into the opening foyer, two uniformed guards ran forward, firing pistols wildly.

Jack and Phil hit the floor, but Max stood his ground, grinning like a maniac. "Jesus Christ, what do they use to train you guys, old episodes of 'Romper Room'?''

His weapon coughed out a splatter of lead, stitching through the attackers, sending up divots of blood and bone.

They crumpled like puppets whose strings had been cut.

Jack and Phil stood up. There were three corridors, leading in three wildly different angles. "Which way?" said Phil.

"That's what I was hoping you'd tell me." Max stalked forward to the fallen mutants. "Ah, looks like Tweedledum and Tweedledee are still sucking oxygen. Observe, guys, your first lesson in mutant interrogation.'' He grabbed one—extremely human-looking, save for the Phantom of the Opera face—by its shock of long green hair. ''Okay, Diaper Rash. Where's this Doc Knox's laboratory? Where's the blond human woman he brought in today?''

''No . . .'' spluttered the mutant. ''Won't tell.''

''Hold him up, Phil.'' Phil stepped forward and grabbed the mutant, keeping him in place with difficulty. Max went over, hoisted the other mutant up, and shoved its face within a foot of the other's. Then he inserted the snub nose of the Uzi into the mutant's mouth. ''Watch carefully, mutie.''

Turkel fired.

The bullets tore through teeth and flesh and bone, splattering out a wild spray of blood. Such was the violence of the assault that the whole top of the mutant's head was torn out. The surviving mutant was splashed with gore. A piece of skin was stuck in his mouth. He spat it out, his eyes widening with horror.

''Got it?'' snarled Turkel, his eyes like a demented demon's. ''That's you in five seconds if I don't hear some directions.''

The mutant began talking.

They walked down a bizarrely canted hallway.

''Aw fuck!'' said Turkel. ''That bastard went and *croaked* on me!'' Disgustedly, he tossed the mutant corpse against the wall. It slid down the wall, leaving a trail of blood, and then limply collapsed to the floor. ''Just when we were getting friendly and all!''

Jack said, ''He told us where to go. That's the important thing.''

''Wish he'd told us where the men's room is,'' said

Phil, looking distinctly green in the gills. "I think I'm going to puke."

"Save it for later. I got the feeling the best is yet to come," said Turkel. "Yeah—that offshoot in that bulby room yonder. That's the door the mutie was talking about. If you're babe's anywhere, kid, she's in there."

Jack Bender did not feel sick at all. Inside, he felt as though he was entirely made of steel, centered by a core of molten lava.

Jenny. Jenny.

"Let's do it," he said grimly.

"Potts, my lad," said Turkel. "You bring up the rear. Any mutants attack from there, you throw up on 'em. That'll take care of 'em."

"Thanks for the vote of confidence."

Beside the door was a panel of buttons. Jack pushed the green one. Green usually indicated "open," at least back at the complex. But nothing happened.

"Stand back, kid. Let me use my Israeli can opener here," said Turkel.

Jack stood back. Max turned the Uzi on the panel and pressed the trigger. The bullets tore the thing up, and sparks flew wildly as insulation burned.

The door slid open.

"Geronimo!" cried Max, hurtling through the smoke. Jack followed immediately, with Phil bringing up the rear.

They stepped into a high-ceilinged room filled with a strange mediciny smell, along with the telltale iron smell of blood.

Standing at a control panel of banks of computers was the mutant known as Dr. Knox.

Off to the side were two mutants, holding machine guns as well.

"Stop where you are!" said Dr. Knox, his bulbous head pulsing like a huge, angry pimple. "Come no further. My assistants are well armed and ready for anything. Norn! Clack! Brandish your weapons!"

The muscular pair showed very large machine guns, stocked with spare rounds of cartridges.

"Yikes," said Turkel. "I know when I'm out-classed!" He turned, gave a broad wink to his companions, then lowered his Uzi.

"That's them!" said Phil. "Those are the muties I saw. The one that took Jenny."

"Where is she?" Jack cried, feeling as though he was losing control of his fear and his rage. "What did you *do* with her, dammit!"

"Ah. I take it you mean the girl. Calm yourself. I assure you that where she is now is quite beyond reach."

Dead?

Was the mutant scientist telling him that Jennifer Anderson, his love, the woman that he was supposed to *bond* with, was . . . dead?

"Bastards!" he screamed and raised his gun.

"Fuck!" cried Turkel, not really expecting this crazy move, but going with it nonetheless, tilting up his Uzi. Phil Potts, not one to be given over to berserker rages, chose caution; he jumped behind a table.

The mutants got off the first burst of fire, but they too had been surprised. A hail of bullets whizzed by Jack's ear, but by then he was aiming and squeezing off rounds with the frenzy of grief.

A slug caught one of the mutants in the abdomen, and reflex tossed the large gun from his hands. He coughed blood and looked up, baffled, at the farmboy wielding the weapon.

Meanwhile, Turkel's Uzi whipped the action, chattering out bullets better aimed than the mutants' were. The upsweep ripped a buzzsaw of lead up the other mutant from groin to face, sprouting a temporary garden of blood. The mutant was thrown back against the computer hard, denting the facade and making his contribution to the research in the interfacing of flesh, blood, and machine.

Screaming wildly, Jack charged closer to the mutant he had only wounded, pumping bullets into his head, splattering it like a ripe pumpkin full of blood.

He caught himself . . . stopped himself.

He wanted to save a couple of bullets in the chamber for the mutant called Dr. Knox . . . The one who had taken Jenny away from him.

He swiveled to face the mutant, who was stabbing wildly at some controls. Before Jack knew what was happening, something whipped into Jack's field of vision, knocking the gun from his hand. He turned and saw this attacker. Some sort of tentacle, like a coil of metal, sprouted from the top of the blocky machine stretching down the wall . . .

And at its tip was a gleaming, razor-sharp scalpel.

It slashed down at him.

Jack flung himself back, and the sharp edge barely nicked his cheek, drawing blood.

"What the hell," said Turkel as more armed metal coils sprang from the computer, whipping down toward him like a maddened metal octopus.

Quickly, Jack switched his sword to the right hand. When the tentacle came back, he swung and caught the scalpel at its base, bending it enough to render it ineffectual. Still, the tentacle was quite effective just for brute strength. It flung him down to the floor.

He was stunned, but not enough to avoid noticing

the flapping of the coattails of Dr. Knox's lab coat as he raced away from the battle. With surprising dexterity, the scientist hurtled onto a nearby table and began to run across it.

"Come back here, you cowardly asshole!" cried Turkel, fending off the whizzing tentacles. "I hear the vat that spawned you was a cesspool for Class Zs."

A gunshot rang through the room.

Startled, Jack turned. Standing up from behind the table was Phil Potts, holding a smoking gun with two hands.

"Good fellow!" cried Turkel dodging a wicked-looking hypodermic. "You winged the bastard. We'll get him now. *I* get to interrogate him."

Dr. Knox, holding a bloody thigh, was teetering out of control on the tabletop. His good leg stepped down on a test tube, causing him to lose his balance. He slammed down onto the surface.

And disappeared.

A splash. A slap of liquid jumping up like a flick of an amoeba's pseudopod. A lull.

He's fallen into some kind of tank, thought Jack.

And then, like a thousand Alka Seltzer tablets, suddenly starting to fizz at once, Dr. Knox exploded back into view.

Or what was left of Dr. Knox.

Most of his face had been eaten away, revealing a grinning skull. The sac holding his excess brain had dissolved, and the brains were leaking out and melting messily. A skeletal hand reached out as though for help, and his jaw opened as though to beg.

The jaw fell off into the liquid.

Slowly, Dr. Knox slipped back into a bubbling, consuming death.

"Goddamn," said Max Turkel, ducking another of

the tentacles. "I've heard about the acidity of my wit, but this is ridiculous!"

"Must have been some kind of disposal tank," said Jack. "Good shot, Phil. You came through."

"Yeah," said Phil. "And I've been watching this computer here. And I think—" He walked over to a safe place and aimed his gun. "I think I've got its number."

In rapid succession he emptied the rest of his .45 into a panel of the computer with a particularly large number of lights. The glowing, colored lights faded, went out like dead Christmas tree lights.

And the tentacles suddenly stopped their attack.

"How the hell did you *do* that?" said Turkel. "Not that I'm not extremely grateful."

"I'm particularly interested in computer technology," said Potts. "I merely logically figured out where the central control node of the mainframe hardware was."

"Max. Do you think that the mutant was telling the truth? Do you think that Jenny's dead?"

"I think we'd better have a look for ourselves. And then—

Suddenly, without warning, the tentacles came back to life. They snaked up and slapped the weapons from the trio's hands, tossing them against the wall, far out of reach.

From the top of the computer, a metallic head perched atop a coil slowly lifted up, glaring down with large, lensed eyes. "Mr. Potts! Surely you've heard of auxiliary power!" it said in a monotone machine voice.

Another door opened, revealing ten Class C mutants, each armed with a seeming arsenal of weapons from handguns through rifles through bazookas.

"Christ, let's get outta here!" said Turkel.

They turned.

Another ten Class C mutants charged through the door, each similarly armed.

"Uhm," said Turkel. "You know, suddenly a nice bubble bath in the Doc's tank over there doesn't seem like such a bad idea."

"No, Maximillian Turkel," a voice like thunder boomed out through the room. "I do not believe that you will be taking a bath again for a long, long time. I suggest that you and your companions drop any hidden weapons now, or there will be no more time at all for any of you."

Into the room stepped a tall mutant, dressed in studded black leather.

"Well, I always wanted to meet you, but never quite this way." Turkel threw down his Uzi. "Boys, I want you to meet BrainGeneral Mordechai Torx."

Frustration welled in Jack Bender like a dark fountain.

Phil Potts threw up.

"All in all," said Max Turkel, hoisting his arms in surrender after tossing a couple of hidden knives onto the floor. "Not one of life's best moments."

CHAPTER 21

"Who are these slugs?" demanded Torx, eyeing Jack and Phil with supreme distaste.

"They appear to be slave workers from the Gamma Farm Complex, BrainGeneral," answered one of his minions.

"Yes. And presumably it has been you two who have been harboring this criminal for two weeks. I'm afraid I have to take Maximillian Turkel to the Emperor Charlemagne. But you—" He put a heavy gloved hand around Jack Bender's neck. The grip felt like a power wrench, tightening. "You two, I shall enjoy killing—"

Jack Bender spat in the creature's scarred face.

"Jesus, Jack!" said Turkel, wincing in his bonds. "I knew you had some rebel in you, but this is ridiculous!"

The BrainGeneral's expression did not change.

His hand did, however. It tightened, and as Jack was securely fastened in handcuffs around his back and ankle chains, he could do nothing.

"Very well, farm slave. Now is as good a time as any!"

A gleam of intense gratification and pleasure appeared in Torx's face. Jack could feel his windpipe close to collapse, and he was growing faint with lack of oxygen.

"Jack! Omigod. JACK!" screamed Phil. A mutant stepped forward and struck the screaming youth down.

Consumed with pain, Jack felt on the verge of unconsciousness.

Just as the light was fading away rapidly, a mutant's cry forced Torx's attention away from his death squeeze.

"BrainGeneral, sir! We have a transmission from Devil's Mountain, New NORAD, Colorado. The Emperor's Headquarters."

"Yes, yes, I know it's the Emperor's Headquarters," said Torx disgustedly. "You want to broadcast it to the world?" He took his hand away from Jack's throat. "Later, slave. Slower," he promised.

Jack's vision faded back on slowly, and he was able to make out the fact that a large screen on the face of the computer had come alive. From it glared an incredibly ugly and incredibly fat face, like a vision from the level of hell reserved for the gluttonous.

"Greetings, my Lord," said the BrainGeneral, essaying a curt bow. "I trust you have a good view of the room."

"Transmission is excellent, thank you, BrainGeneral Torx," said the thing, lips and jowls flapping loosely.

"Gosh," said Phil Potts. "It's the Emperor Charlemagne himself!"

"Yes, in living ugly," muttered Turkel.

The BrainGeneral said, "Then you can see that I have caputured the rebel Maximillian Turkel, as well as two of his cohorts."

"Yes, and about time, too, Torx. I can expect to

see you and the subhuman rebel back by tomorrow then.''

"We shall fly back tonight. I have already commandeered a jet from the nearest air base. Maximillian Turkel should be in your hands by late in the morning.''

"Good. Very good. Subhuman Turkel! I look forward to personally overseeing your demise. You have caused me a great deal of stress, anxiety, and trouble.''

"Glad to know it, Charlie. Oh, and by the way, I like hot and cold running water in my room and poached eggs for breakfast.''

"A defiant one, eh, Torx? I knew he would be the source of great amusement. Do you think he shall make jokes even as his cells scream out for death?''

"A most fascinating thought. I shall enjoy finding out as well,'' said Torx. "But in the meantime, would it amuse you to watch the deaths of his accomplices now?''

"What? Those farm workers there? No, I don't want them dead, Torx.''

"What?'' said Torx, stunned.

"BrainGeneral Torx, I have, over the conduits of my network, been receiving reports of your activities through the area. Your procedures seem a tad too bloodthirsty to maintain the status quo properly among the halfsies. While I am extremely pleased that you have captured Turkel and will certainly consider a reward, I cannot condone the senseless slaying of two accomplices he must have coerced into accompanying him!''

"Damned straight,'' said Turkel. "Told 'em to come along with me or I'd blow their heads off. If it weren't for the shitheads, I'd have been over the hill

192

by now, but they held me back. Mutant-sucking bastards!'' he screamed at Jack and Phil.

''Wha—!'' cried Torx. However, he immediately stifled himself, even though it was clear to Jack that he was close to bursting with anger and frustration. ''Very well, Your Excellency. Your wish is my command.'' A bow.

''Good. And thus, I show the mercy of the Emperor. However, we cannot entirely take this without blinking. I shall personally notify their immediate supervisor that they are to be checked into a Personality Rehab Department at the earliest covenience for, ah, reprogramming.''

Jack's heart sank whatever few inches it had to go to rock bottom. Personality Rehab was virtually a memory wipe, with a neurochemical scrape to make sure there were no bits and pieces left. Reprogramming, of course, was the installation of a new person—but in all the cases that Jack had seen, the person had been converted into a total robot. Human beings were lucky in that the process was lengthy and expensive, or the muties probably would have done it to them all.

''Yes, Your Excellency. Is that all?'' said Torx tersely.

''That is all for now.'' The head turned, its bulging eyes rolling absurdly to the main prisoner. ''Maximillian Turkel! I look forward to . . . *playing* with you after your arrival tomorrow.''

''Tennis, I hope! Or squash? And I'm excellent at racquetball. Or how about mutant football? Looks like your back would make a good-sized field.''

The fat face twitched. ''We will see how well your wit fares with your tongue ripped out and jammed up a ventral orifice!''

The transmission ended.

"Great way to get the last word in a conversation," said Turkel seriously. "Hey, Torx. Guess this means that if I don't make it to see the Emperor Charlemagne in one piece, your ass is in a crack!"

Torx turned, eyes glaring at Jack Bender. "I am not easily thwarted. I take satisfaction only in knowing that you will, for all practical purposes, be nullified."

"There's many a slip between cup and lip, mutant," said Jack, meeting the BrainGeneral glare for glare.

"Oooh! Jack! I haven't heard that one for years. And you know, Torxy pal, it's so true."

"Silence." The mutant stepped up to Jack Bender, shaking his ferociously ugly head. "I perceive a curious fire in you, young subhuman. Perhaps if all your fellows had your spirit, they would not be the vassals and slime that they are. But we cannot afford such spirit, Jack Bender. Such spirit must be snuffed out like candles, before the conflagration can grow! There is a brave and wonderful world for us post-humans of this world, and for our descendants—"

One of the subservients suddenly ran up to Torx and whispered something into his ear.

His eyes grew wide, and the faintest of tremors shook him. Jack read a flash of tremendous disappointment in those normally dead eyes—and then the black curtains closed again.

He looked over to the tank, then to the computer. Then BrainGeneral Torx regarded Jack with total deadness.

"I would trade all my wealth to kill you all this instant," he whispered. "This will have to suffice my wrath."

He stepped forward and struck Jack in the face with his fist.

Unconsciousness closed around Jack Bender, its claws unsheathed.

CHAPTER 22

It was a time of dreamless black.

It covered Jack Bender like the heaviest of tars, and when he emerged it clung tenaciously to the edges of his vision.

Something had woken him up. Something familiar.

His jaw hurt. It hurt bad. It hurt so bad, he barely noticed the tremendous headache he had, to say nothing of aches in every joint in his body.

Suddenly a cold splash of water impacted with his face, and he realized that it was identical to the sensation that had dragged him up out of the tar pit.

"Wake up!" cried a nasal, grating little voice. "Wake up, Bender!"

That voice. He recognized it. Jack blinked, and he realized that he was blinking back water.

That was what had woken him up. Water. *Cold* water.

"Wha' happ—" he slurred. "Where am I?"

"Still up the creek," said Phil Potts in a strained voice. "Still without a paddle."

Jack tried to sit up, but he could not. He realized that he was on the ground—half cement, and half tarp. The familiar smells of oil and gasoline tickled his nostrils. The blurry forms were familiar, and with a start he realized that they were in the machine shop of the Gamma Farm Complex.

But what where they doing there?

"Ah," said that annoying, persistent voice again. "Finally, he's awake. Maybe we can get somewhere now."

Jack turned his head, and slowly his eyesight brought the speaker into focus.

It was Brown. Brown 46. Their supervisor. What was Brown 46 doing standing over them in the machine shop?

And then it came back to him, all of it. The institute. The raid. BrainGeneral Torx. The Emperor . . .

And most of all, Jenny.

"Jenny!" he said, still not quite all there. "Have to save Jenny! Have to—"

"Save your futile wishes, Bender. Jenny Anderson is dead. Dead, dead, dead, and dead!"

That woke Jack up. Furiously, he lurched toward the perpetrator of this filth, these lies.

But he was brought up short by the cuffs on his wrists and ankles. He fell face forward onto cement. He could feel a split lip reopen and taste fresh blood seeping into his mouth.

"Jenny," he said. "How do you . . . know . . . that Jenny . . . is dead?"

"Because that was what they told me they'd do to her, Bender. I watched them once, just for the show. It was most interesting. This was Hazel, Hazel Larkin that I watched. The show was very entertaining. Shall I tell you about it?"

"What are you doing to us, Brown?" demanded Potts. "I thought we were supposed to be rehabilitated?"

"Oh, yes, and you shall be. The van is scheduled

197

to come and pick you up tomorrow morning. But in the meantime, I thought I'd *play* for a bit.'' Brown reached over to a workbench and grabbed something that brought instinctive terror to Jack. It was a long cylindrical device with a rubber handle and a metal end. Wires ran along the shaft.

The prod.

The electric prod, Brown's favorite method for punishment.

There was not a soul among the human slaves who had not had a taste of the exquisite pain Supervisor Brown dished out through his electric prod. He tended to use it mostly in the earlier years of a slave's life, to properly indoctrinate him. Somehow, Jack had avoided the prod for the last few years, principally because he was such a good worker and the use of the prod tended to make the victim withdraw for a while, and Brown had discovered that withdrawn workers produced very little. But the very sight of the thing was enough to make Jack cringe and shrink away reflexively.

Brown said, ''You see, I'm upset with you, Potts and Bender. For two reasons. First, because you have betrayed me. But then you are slaves, and that happens from time to time. However, what angers me the most is that I am losing two of my best workers! My quota will be down for this year.''

''Uhm,'' said Potts, eyeing the prod with the same fear that Jack felt. ''Well, we won't exactly be here, but they'll bring the rehabs back.''

''Right. And what about Abrahams and Martin? Practically useless. They're maybe good for kitchen duty and often as not they pee in their own pants. No, boys, you have not only done a terrible thing to the Cause, you have hurt me irrevocably.'' A faint smile touched Brown's swollen lips. "And now I'm going to hurt you."

"I have an idea," said Potts. "Tell you what, Brownie. You get us off of the rehab stuff, and we'll work *twice* as hard."

The mutant just ignored him. He started toward Jack, the prod waving in his hand like some magic wand.

"But I didn't finish about what happened to Hazel Larkin—and what they did to Jennifer Anderson. Well, Hazel was pretty well chewed up—apparently she'd tried to escape. So they strapped her down and they took a nice sharp surgical saw. They buzzed through her skull, Bender. And they took out her *brain*. What for, I haven't the faintest. Ever wonder about Jennifer Anderson's brain, Bender, as you two rutted away? Oh, yes, I would watch you sometimes in the linen closet, through a special peephole. Most entertaining . . ."

Jack squirmed, his fear of the prod gone. Now he just wanted to get his hands on Brown's throat, any way he could.

"Ever wonder what color Jennifer Anderson's brains were? Hazel's were sort of red and gray—"

"You'd better kill me, Brown. Because, I swear to God, I'm going to come back, rehab or no rehab, and kill you."

"Oh dear me! I'm shaking in my boots. Why don't you shake along with me."

Brown touched Jack's chest with the prod. The shock went right into his lungs, making it difficult to breathe. The pain was excruciating. Jack screamed.

"What? What did you say? Voltage not high enough, Bender? Okay. I'll just up it a tad. Try this on for size."

Giggling, the mutant touched Jack's abdomen.

Jack screamed again, writhing in his chains. But he did not beg. When Brown started in with the prod, you were supposed to beg him to stop. That was a part of the game. But Jack Bender was damned if he was going to beg this time.

"Oh, yes, ticklish huh? Well, let's see what happens when I put this little lovely just a little bit *lower!*" A fiendish glint in his eye, the mutant lowered the prod toward Jack Bender's testicles.

Jack steeled himself.

What happened next was a blur.

One moment, Brown was hovering over Jack. The next moment, something flew out of the periphery of Jack's pain-dulled vision.

Brown grunted, fell to his knees, and then keeled over.

Jack looked up. Standing over him was Phil Potts, holding a large wrench in his hands.

In his cuffless hands.

"Phil," said Jack. "Phil . . . how . . ."

"I gotta get the key," Phil said. "The bastard must have the key in one of his pockets. They'd have given him the key to these things, don't you think, Jack?" Potts shuffle-hopped over to the fallen mutant and began going through his pockets; Jack could see that Phil still had the ankle restraints.

"Phil," he said dully, fighting off the catatonia the prod always produced. "How . . . How did . . ."

"What, get out of the cuffs? Well, only one actually." He held up a hand, and the cuff dangled off his wrist. "I had thrown up on it. The vomit made my hand slick. I got skinny hands, and I've always been able to contort them. So I slipped out back at the lab. Had to hide it till the right moment. Which was now."

"Whew! You saved my bacon!"

"Just glad old Brownie didn't come for me first, that's all I can say. Ah, here it is!" Potts pulled a key from one of the mutant's pockets. "Let's see if this works."

"If it doesn't, we'll just have to use one of the saws here."

"On these babies? They look like tungsten plus to me. No, I think—" There was a satisfying *click*. "Ah ha!" The ankle bracelets fell off. Rapidly, Phil attended to Jack. In just a few moments, Jack was up, rubbing his wrists.

"That's *much* better."

The mutant on the floor groaned and stirred.

"What about Brownie?"

"Hold him down, Phil."

"Sure."

Jack went to the workbench and got an oil can. He squeezed it. Black oil squirted plentifully. He went back to where Phil Potts was sitting on the mutant supervisor, bent over, and picked up the electric prod.

Brown groaned again. His eyelids seemed to be trying to open, but were unsuccessful at the chore.

"Okay," said Jack. "Let's get his pants off."

"What?" said Phil. "I don't wanna see what's underneath Brownie's pants!"

"Well, presumably there's an asshole. And that's where this," said Jack, shaking the prod, ". . . where this little thing is going to go!"

"Boy," said Potts, his eyes gleaming with excitement. "Talk about fantasies fulfilled."

"Yeah. So get the pants off!"

Phil started working on the belt. Brownie opened his eyes. Disorientation showed in him, then realization. And with the realization of the spot he was in, pure fear invaded them as well.

For a moment, something human showed in the mutant's expression . . .

"Please. Please don't hurt me."

And it broke Jack Bender's anger and resolve.

He threw the prod over into the corner. "Forget it, Potts. I can't do it."

"Huh?"

But then Brown started to struggle, and Potts had to work hard to keep him pinned to the ground.

"You slime! You cess! You'll pay for this!" screeched Brown. "Help! Help!"

"We'd better tie him up, and quickly," said Potts. "I'll get something."

Jack had no sooner turned to go back to the workbench for some rope and a gag, than somehow Brown was able to free a hand.

"Jack! Jack!"

Jack turned just in time to see Brown punch Potts hard in the face. Potts, dazed, fell off the mutant, and with surprising quickness, Brown got to his feet and started to run for the door.

"Jack! Get him. If he gets out, he'll bring back help!"

Jack started running, but all the effort and the pain of the day had sapped his speed.

Brown dodged one of Jack's seeding machines and headed for the door. "You'll pay! You shits will *pay!*"

There was only one hope. Jack jumped on the seeding machine. It could go faster than he could now. He punched the ignition button. The motor roared to life.

Thank God he'd fixed it up.

Brown had reached the doors, but he'd latched them

from the inside and was having a hard time unlatching them. He fumbled at the locks, so desperate to get out that his coordination was off.

Jack engaged the gears and strip-shifted the thing up to twenty-five miles an hour in fifteen seconds.

Thank God he was a mechanic. Thank God he was a hot rodder at heart!

Finally, Brown flung off the latch. He pushed open the door and began to run out into the open.

However, it was too late. No sooner had he stepped outside than the seeder caught up with him.

No mercy this time, thought Jack Bender. This time their lives depended on ruthlessness.

The seeder ran over the mutant.

It caught him so quickly, he didn't have time to even yell.

There was a sickening thud, and then Brown was under the wheels.

Fwuck fwuck fwuck! came worse sounds from beneath the machine as it rolled over the supervisor.

Blood splattered and gushed in livid spurts.

With one more hard bump, the machine's back wheels ran over the mutant. Jack put on the brakes and turned off the engine, so that no more noise than necessary would echo through the complex. He just prayed that Brown's cries had not been heard. Most likely not; the mutant supervisor had probably chosen the mechanics shop specifically because it was fairly soundproof. Brown hadn't wanted the screams from the torture he intended to wake anybody up.

The intent, it would seem, had backfired on him.

Phil Potts was standing over the mutant.

"Jesus," he said, staring down.

"Is he still alive?"

"Uh—no, he looks kind of *dead* to me!"

Brown's body lay sprawled on the cement. The head had been crushed like a melon of blood. Large chunks had been dug from the body, leaving gaping holes in which soybeans had been planted.

"The seeder was on."

Phil looked up from the soggy, gory mess that had been their mutant supervisor.

"How unnecessary," he said, shaking his head and smiling sardonically. "Brown 46 wasn't worth beans."

EPILOGUE

When dawn began threatening over the horizon, Jack Bender was ready.

However, Phil Potts wasn't.

"I don't know," said the lanky youth, staring grimly at the plane. "I still say we should have just started running."

"I told you not to worry, Phil," Jack said. He sipped the last bit of his coffee and then got up to check the supplies one last time. "I had a takeoff with Turkel. He taught me. He says I'm a natural flier. Anyway, you've got those books. Besides being navigator and plotting our course and all, if there's any problem, we can just look it up. I admit there are a few gauges on the dashboard I don't quite understand yet, but I'm a quick study. Especially with mechanical stuff. It'll all work out, you'll see. Come on now. We had to wait till dawn because at this point flying in the dark isn't a good idea. But if we wait any longer, there's a big chance the muties are going to be all over the place, with heavy artillery. We've got a few hours till the rehab van shows and they realize that we're gone."

They'd cleaned up the trashed mess that was Brown 46, then hosed down the cement. Then they'd sneaked into Potts's hidden library, gotten the books and some other stuff that Potts said they needed.

Then they'd gone to the plane.

Jack had figured that it really wasn't a good idea to hide in his tree house; there was always the possibility that the previously lax mutants might indeed know of its existence, and if they caught them in it, there'd be no place to go. Besides, the closer to the plane the better. If they had to take off at night, then so be it.

Another factor was Jack's exhaustion. No way was he going to be able to fly a plane with this kind of fatigue. He needed some rest, and he needed it badly. So after they stored the extra supplies and Jack had clamped the fuel line back into place while Phil held a flashlight (fuck Turkel!—that was all that the thing needed, a clamp!), they took turns with watches while the other caught some shut-eye.

Now, Phil Potts was staring at the plane with extreme disquiet. "What if I'm airsick? What if I throw up?"

"Just open a window and stick your head out."

"Look, Jack. Do we really have to do this?"

"I don't think we really have much choice now, do we, Phil? We've *got* to get out of here!"

"No. I mean—the other stuff. I mean, it makes more sense to go, like, north. There are rumors of free zones in parts of Canada and Alaska where the muties leave halfsies and humans pretty much alone."

"Yeah, I know . . . 'cause it's so cold up there and they don't want it. No, Phil. I have to do this."

"But Colorado, Jack! Rescue Max Turkel from the stronghold of Emperor Charlemagne! Ever hear of the Japanese kamikaze pilots of World War II? They had a better chance of survival than we do if we carry out this crazy plan."

Jack shook his head. "Phil. Max Turkel could have just told me to go fuck myself and take off in this plane and have been scot-free now. Instead, he helped me try and get Jenny back. Well, that didn't work out, and now that BrainGeneral Turds or whatever his name is has him and—" Jack took a deep breath. "Phil, all this time you've talked about rebellion, you've been right and I've been wrong."

Phil blinked. "Uhm . . . well, you know, Jack, you could maybe have been a *little* right!"

"Nope. I was totally wrong. And that bastard Turkel . . . I hate to say this, but I should have listened to him. Maybe Jenny would have been alive now if I had .."

"Jack, you know, his number was about up anyway, and maybe we really should rethink this thing and—"

"You want to stay here, Pottsie?"

"Uhm . . ." Phil Potts said sheepishly. "No, not really."

"Then get your rebel ass in that plane. I'm telling you, I'm a *natural* pilot. We'll have the bugs worked out within an *hour.*"

"But how about landing?"

"We'll worry about that later."

Phil Potts swallowed. "Yeah. I guess you're right, Jack. Sorry. Morning isn't the best time for me. Maybe I'll feel better later." He climbed up into the cockpit and closed his door.

"Buckle up, pal!" said Jack.

"Uhm . . . what about parachutes?"

"What are parachutes?"

Phil Potts sighed heavily and closed his eyes, resigning himself to his fate.

Jack walked around to the front of the plane, pausing for a moment to look back toward the east where light was pouring up from the horizon and where the farm complex and his old life lay. He felt the bandage on his neck, and a shiver of excitement coursed down his spine.

He looked west. That was the direction that Phil had said that Colorado was. And that was where that plane was taking Max Turkel right at this moment.

"Max, you asshole," he whispered under his breath. "Stay alive. We're coming to get you."

And then Jack Bender walked around the other side of the plane and hoisted himself behind the controls.

SPECIAL PREVIEW!

Here is an
exciting scene from

MUTANTS AMOK #2:

MUTANT HELL

On sale now!

When Jack Bender punched the ignition button for the small plane and the engine coughed and spat and refused to start, he knew he and Phil Potts were in trouble.

However, when a shot rang out and a bullet whizzed over the cabin—that was when he knew they were really in deep shit.

"Halt!" cried a garbled voice over a sputtering megaphone. "Halt in the name of Emperor Charlemagne!"

"Don't look now, but we've got ourself a member of the Royal Mounted Mutant Police at twelve o'clock high!" said Potts.

"That's why you've got a gun, Pottsie," Jack said through gritted teeth. "Deal with him!" He tried the button again. What the hell was going on here?

Phil grimly pushed back a window of the small plane and shoved his .45 out. Jack Bender, not wanting to flood the engine, gave it a rest and hazarded a look behind them.

Sure enough, coming up on a horse, dressed in a bright red and green uniform was a Class N mutant. A Lawkeeper. You didn't see too many Lawkeepers around the Iowa Gamma Farm Complex, but when you did, you remembered them. And Jack sure as hell remembered the ones *he* saw. They were virtual slabs of muscle, but not like Class A mutants, the frontliners originally vatted to war for humanity. No, they were molded more along the line of Southern sheriffs, with gigantic abdomens bulging and reflector sunglass-goggles permanently welded to silicon-reinforced skin. These large abdomens they used to holster weapons, personal cellular radios and the bottles of Spudweiser, a cheap mutant beer they favored. Jack had only seen Lawkeepers when one of the enslaved humans had killed another for some reason, a very rare occasion.

What would Max Turkel do in a situation like this?

Probably curse and run like hell.

The explosion of the .45 Magnum in the small cabin was deafening, and the recoil slammed Phil back against the wall. Although the bullet went wild, it served its purpose. The mutant cop slowed his horse and went for cover behind a nearby tree. Class Ns were not kamikaze, like certain warrior classes. They were designed by BrainGeneral scientists for smarts and cunning as well as brawn and weapons expertise. You fired a .45 at them, the suckers ducked.

That was all fine by Jack Bender. It bought him a little more time to get the plane started.

"Damn!" said Potts, rubbing his tousled head of brown hair. "I did myself more damage than I did him!"

"Keep on trying! Shoot the bastard!" said Jack.

"Calm down, calm down! We'll never get off the ground with you having a panic attack." But Potts obediently stuck the weapon out the window again. "Must have discovered old Brownie was missing." Brownie was Brown the Fourth, Point Six, their mutant overseer whom Jack had run over with a seeding machine. "Must have discovered *we* were missing."

"No shit, Sherlock."

"Hey, that's *my* line. I'm the book reader!"

"Just shoot the mutant!"

"Okay, okay! Just get this thing off the ground."

Pottsie hadn't been so much in a hurry to fly with an inexperienced pilot just a few minutes ago. Now, though, with a gun-toting mutant breathing fire down his neck, he suddenly longed for the clouds.

Jack was about to push the starter button and try it again when, in a flash of revelation, he realized what was wrong. God, he'd been so stupid! He'd helped Max Turkel work on this plane after it had wrecked on the complex two weeks ago, and he'd personally fixed the engine. It was so old-fashioned, so primitive, even most of the farm complex machinery was more advanced. This engine had a *manual* choke, whereas he was used to an *automatic*.

He fumbled for the thing, pulled it out, gave the accelerator some steady gas, and punched the starter button again.

The engine coughed, turned over, caught, revved. The propeller spun quickly toward a blur. Almost immediately, Jack could feel the pull, but held the brakes to build up some power first.

Phil Potts's .45 exploded again, slamming another bullet toward the mutant policeman. Potts had braced himself this time, so he didn't slam back so hard. "Rats!" he cried. "Missed him! But I got the tree, Jack! I was close!"

"Well, keep him behind it! Give me just twenty more seconds and we'll be on our way."

"Right. I—Oh, Jeez! He's charging!"

Jack had time to look, so he swiveled around in his

seat straining at the seat belt. Sure enough, the mutant cop was running toward them, having left his horse behind. But Class Ns weren't suppossed to do such foolhardy stuff.

And then Jack saw it. The guy had some sort of reinforced plastic shield he was holding in front of him. Christ, all he had to do was to get off a couple of lucky shots to punch a hole in something vital in the plane.

"Give me the gun!" he said.

"But Jack . . ."

"I said, 'Give me the *gun!*'" Jack yelled.

Potts handed over the gun. Jack had his own gun, but it would take time to pull it out and ready it. They had no time. Jack took no time to aim. He just fired. The bullet went wide, but it served Jack's purpose well enough. The mutant policeman had been bringing around his own gun—a .44 service revolver from the looks of it—and he had to withdraw it and stop in his tracks to hide behind the riot plastic. Meanwhile, the propeller was working up some speed.

However, the cop didn't stay down long. As soon as the bullet whistled away overhead, he had his ugly pig nose out and was oinking away toward them, little eyes flaring in a broad, fat, intent face.

Damn. Seconds more! That was all he needed! *Seconds* more!

He fired again. This time, though, he aimed.

The shield was jumping up and down with the mutant cop's jogging gait. The bullet passed over its top on a downswing. The .45 mm hollow-point shell crashed full bore into the officer's reinforced skin and skull, punching through despite the obstacles straight into his unreinforced brain, the spreading shrapnel doing a Mixmaster number on the gray matter, rendering it the consistency of oatmeal. The bullet pieces did not exit, but rather ricocheted around inside the skull, turning the brain into total slag.

Pumping blood from his forehead like a firehose, the cop was hurled back into the grass. A few leg spasms later, the mutant cop was not only down, but thoroughly dead and still.

Potts said, "Damn, Jack! Good shooting!"

Jack said nothing. He tossed the hot, smoking gun onto his friend's lap, and then let go of the brakes.

The propeller tugged them into instant forward motion. Too bad he didn't have a runway for his first solo takeoff, thought Jack. All he had was a flat field—and not a whole hell of a lot of that.

Still, he managed to keep the Piper Cub from nosing down despite its abrupt and unconventional start, and even though this was his first time behind the controls of a plane after his run-through under the tutelage of Max Turkel, his instinct was correct—he felt as though the controls were a part of his body.

He was a natural flier.

Still, that didn't mean that when the wheels left the ground things were exactly steady, and Phil Potts supplied the appropriate sound effects.

"Yikes!" and "Oh Jesus!" and "Oh my God, we're going to crash!"

Jack said, "Shut up!" and fought to steady the wings.

"We're going to hit those trees!"

Jack pulled the stick harder, pushing the wing flaps down to their maximum angle, pushing the small plane. The engine sputtered and coughed.

"Jack!" cried Potts. "Jack, be careful. You're stalling it! You're too steep!"

But it was either chance a stall or slam into those oaks, so Jack just kept on doing what he was doing.

The plane's wheels brushed the topmost leaves of the smallest oak. Jack gave it two seconds, and then lowered a bit, tilting the wings to pull around. The plane responded like a kite to a pull of its master's hand on the string; it swung around perfectly. Jack leveled it off, veering around and picking up speed to climb some more, crossing the field from which they had taken off in doing so.

Phil said, "Holy shit, Jack. Look down there!"

Jack took a quick look and he took in a quick breath.

Mutants.

A *horde* of mutants. Some, like the first that they had dealt with, were on horseback. Others were in cars and trucks. Even as Jack turned his attention back to the controls of the plane, a megaphoned voice reached up to grab him about the ears like a teacher boxing a student.

"Jack Bender!" it cried. "Philip Potts. We know that you are up there in that flying vehicle. Return immediately and be disciplined!"

"Yeah, sure," said Phil, getting his .45 ready again. "Only this time it's not the personality rehab for us—it's the axe, right?"

"Save the ammunition, Phil," said Jack, tilting the flaps and sending the punchy little plane higher. "I just want to get out of here."

The mutants weren't saving their ammunition, however. They gave the plane virtually no time to obey the strident orders before a hail of bullets popped below, a few whizzing past the cabin uncomfortably close. From below, a howitzer barked; a grenade exploded just below them, rocking the plane with its shock wave.

"My God, where'd they get the heavy artillery?" Phil said.

"A detachment of BrainGeneral Torx's men must have stayed behind," shouted Jack. "All the more reason to split as quickly as possible!"

"I just hope they don't send jet fighters or helicopters or whatever other high-tech equipment they've got in the area after us!"

Jack said nothing. He just grimly fought for altitude. He didn't even want to think about that possibility right now. Because if the mutants had some kind of modern aircraft loaded with high-tech weapons nearby—well, that was all she wrote for Phil and him.

No. It wouldn't happen, it *couldn't* happen. Jack wouldn't let it, he had a task to perform. He was going to avenge the death of Jennifer Anderson at the hands of BrainGeneral Torx. And, most importantly, he was going to rescue the rebel leader Maximillian Turkel from his mutant captives. He had to. He had *sworn* to.

Amid the storm and hail of bullets and explosives cast after them by the mutant forces below, Jack hurled the little plane at its top speed west, toward Colorado, toward the Mountain, toward the mutant hell where the demon BrainGeneral Torx had taken Turkel.

I'm coming Max, he thought grimly. I'm coming.

Avon Books presents your worst nightmares—

...haunted houses

ADDISON HOUSE 75587-4/$4.50 US/$5.95 Can
Clare McNally

THE ARCHITECTURE OF FEAR
70553-2/$3.95 US/$4.95 Can
edited by Kathryn Cramer & Peter D. Pautz

...unspeakable evil

HAUNTING WOMEN 89881-0/$3.95 US/$4.95 Can
edited by Alan Ryan

TROPICAL CHILLS 75500-9/$3.95 US/$4.95 Can
edited by Tim Sullivan

...blood lust

THE HUNGER 70441-2/$4.50 US/$5.95 Can
THE WOLFEN 70440-4/$4.50 US/$5.95 Can
Whitley Strieber